THE SMURF REPORTER

Peyo

THE SMURF REPORTER

That Chef Smurf ought to be more careful! He's working too much!
?
Peyew! This trash smurfs really bad! Hup, here it goes in the trashcan!
!
Yuck!
Soon after, at the press...
Don't make faces, Greedy Smurf! A real reporter's got to smurf a scoop no matter what the cost!
And this one will get Smurfs talking!
RUB
RUB

A SMURFS GRAPHIC NOVEL BY Peyo

WITH THE COLLABORATION OF
LUC PARTHOENS AND THIERRY CULLIFORD – SCRIPT
LUDO BORECKI – ART
NINE AND JOSÉ GRANDMONT – COLOR

PAPERCUTZ™
NEW YORK

SMURFS GRAPHIC NOVELS AVAILABLE FROM PAPERCUTZ™

PURPLE SMURFS
THE SMURFS AND THE MAGIC FLUTE
THE SMURF KING
SMURFETTE
THE SMURFS AND THE EGG
THE SMURFS AND THE HOWLIBIRD
ASTRO SMURF
SMURF APPRENTICE
GARGAMEL AND THE SMURFS
THE RETURN OF THE SMURFETTE
THE SMURF OLYMPICS
SMURF VS SMURF
SMURF SOUP

THE BABY SMURF
SMURFLINGS
AEROSMURF
LAZY SMURF
THE FINANCE SMURF
THE JEWEL SMURFER
DOCTOR SMURF
THE WILD SMURF
THE SMURF MENACE
CAN'T SMURF PROGRESS
SMURFS CHRISTMAS
FOREVER SMURFETTE
SMURFS MONSTERS
SMURFS

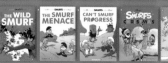

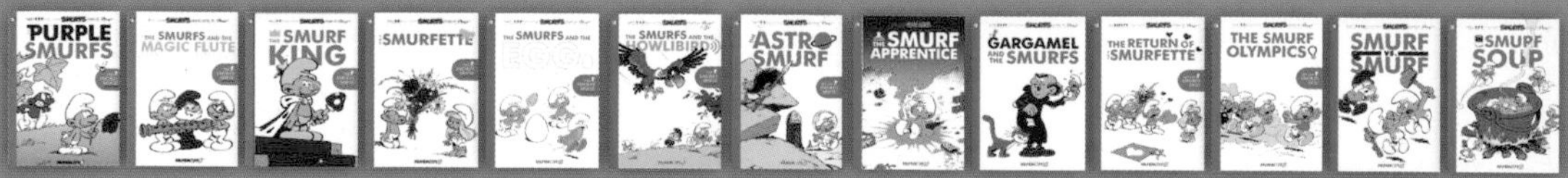

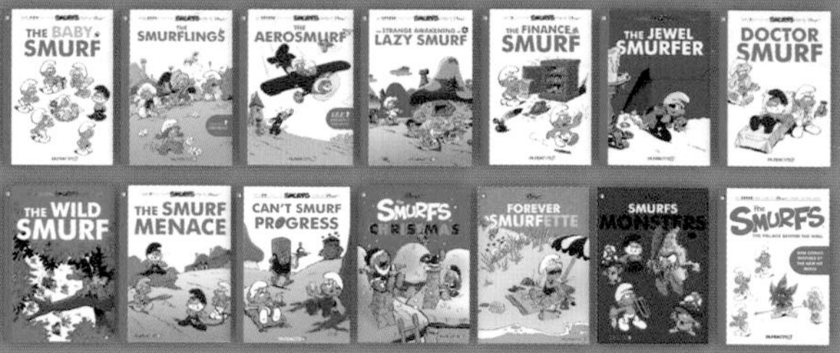

1. **THE PURPLE SMURFS**
2. **THE SMURFS AND THE MAGIC FLUTE**
3. **THE SMURF KING**
4. **THE SMURFETTE**
5. **THE SMURFS AND THE EGG**
6. **THE SMURFS AND THE HOWLIBIRD**
7. **THE ASTROSMURF**
8. **THE SMURF APPRENTICE**
9. **GARGAMEL AND THE SMURFS**
10. **THE RETURN OF THE SMURFETTE**
11. **THE SMURF OLYMPICS**
12. **SMURF VS. SMURF**
13. **SMURF SOUP**
14. **THE BABY SMURF**
15. **THE SMURFLINGS**
16. **THE AEROSMURF**
17. **THE STRANGE AWAKENING OF LAZY SMURF**
18. **THE FINANCE SMURF**
19. **THE JEWEL SMURFER**
20. **DOCTOR SMURF**
21. **THE WILD SMURF**
22. **THE SMURF MENACE**
23. **CAN'T SMURF PROGRESS**
24. **THE SMURF REPORTER**

- **THE SMURF CHRISTMAS**
- **FOREVER SMURFETTE**
- **SMURFS MONSTERS**
- **THE VILLAGE BEHIND THE WALL**

THE SMURFS graphic novels are available in paperback for $5.99 each and in hardcover for $10.99 each, except for THE SMURFS #21-#23, and THE VILLAGE BEHIND THE WALL, which are $7.99 in paperback and $12.99 in hardcover, at booksellers everywhere. You can also order online at papercutz.com. Or call 1-800-886-1223, Monday through Friday, 9 – 5 EST. MC, Visa, and AmEx accepted. To order by mail, please add $4.00 for postage and handling for first book ordered, $1.00 for each additional book and make check payable to NBM Publishing. Send to:
Papercutz, 160 Broadway, Suite 700, East Wing, New York, NY 10038.

THE SMURFS graphic novels are also available digitally wherever e-books are sold.

PAPERCUTZ.COM

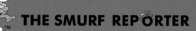

THE SMURF REPORTER

"The Smurf Reporter"
*BY PEYO
WITH THE COLLABORATION OF
LUC PARTHOENS AND THIERRY CULLIFORD FOR THE SCRIPT,
LUDO BORECKI FOR ARTWORK,
NINE AND JOSÉ GRANDMONT FOR COLORS.*

"The Flute Smurfers"
*BY PEYO
WITH THE COLLABORATION OF
LUC PARTHOENS AND THIERRY CULLIFORD FOR THE SCRIPT,
JEROEN DE CONINCK FOR ARTWORK,
NINE CULLIFORD FOR COLORS.*

Joe Johnson, *SMURFLATIONS*
Bryan Senka, *LETTERING SMURF*
Matt. Murray, *SMURF CONSULTANT*
Dawn Guzzo, *SMURFIC DESIGN*
Jeff Whitman, *ASSISTANT MANAGING SMURF*
Jim Salicrup, *SMURF-IN-CHIEF*

*HARDCOVER EDITION ISBN: 978-1-6299-1851-8
PAPERBACK EDITION ISBN: 978-1-6299-1850-1*

PRINTED IN KOREA MAY 2019

Papercutz books may be purchased for business or promotional use. For information on bulk purchases please contact Macmillan Corporate and Premium Sales Department at (800) 221-7945 x5442.

*DISTRIBUTED BY MACMILLAN
SECOND PAPERCUTZ PRINTING*

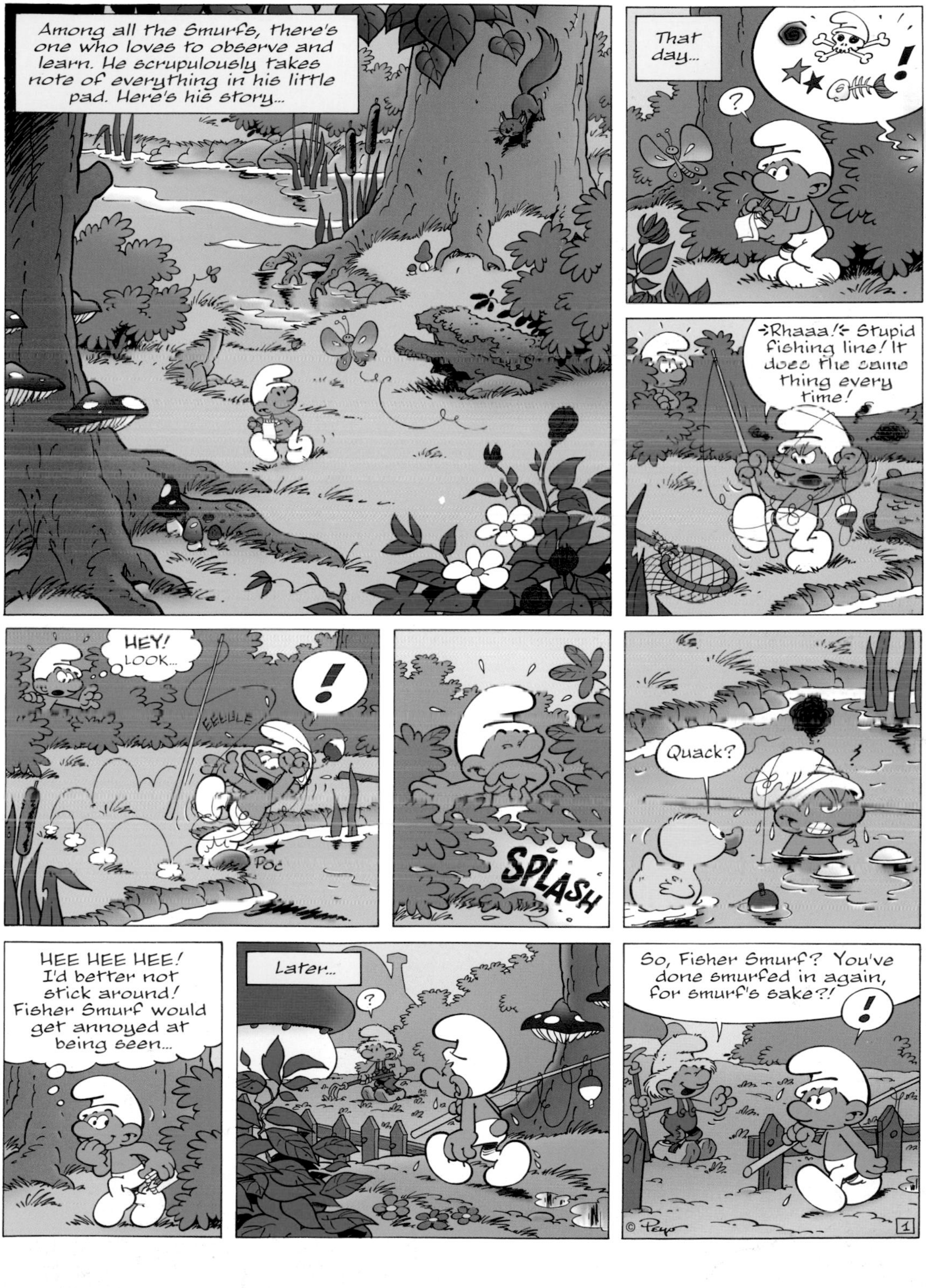

Among all the Smurfs, there's one who loves to observe and learn. He scrupulously takes note of everything in his little pad. Here's his story...
That day...
?
!
Rhaaa! Stupid fishing line! It does the same thing every time!
HEY! LOOK...
EEEUUE
!
POC
SPLASH
Quack?
HEE HEE HEE! I'd better not stick around! Fisher Smurf would get annoyed at being seen...
Later...
?
So, Fisher Smurf? You've done smurfed in again, for smurf's sake?!
!
© Peyo
1

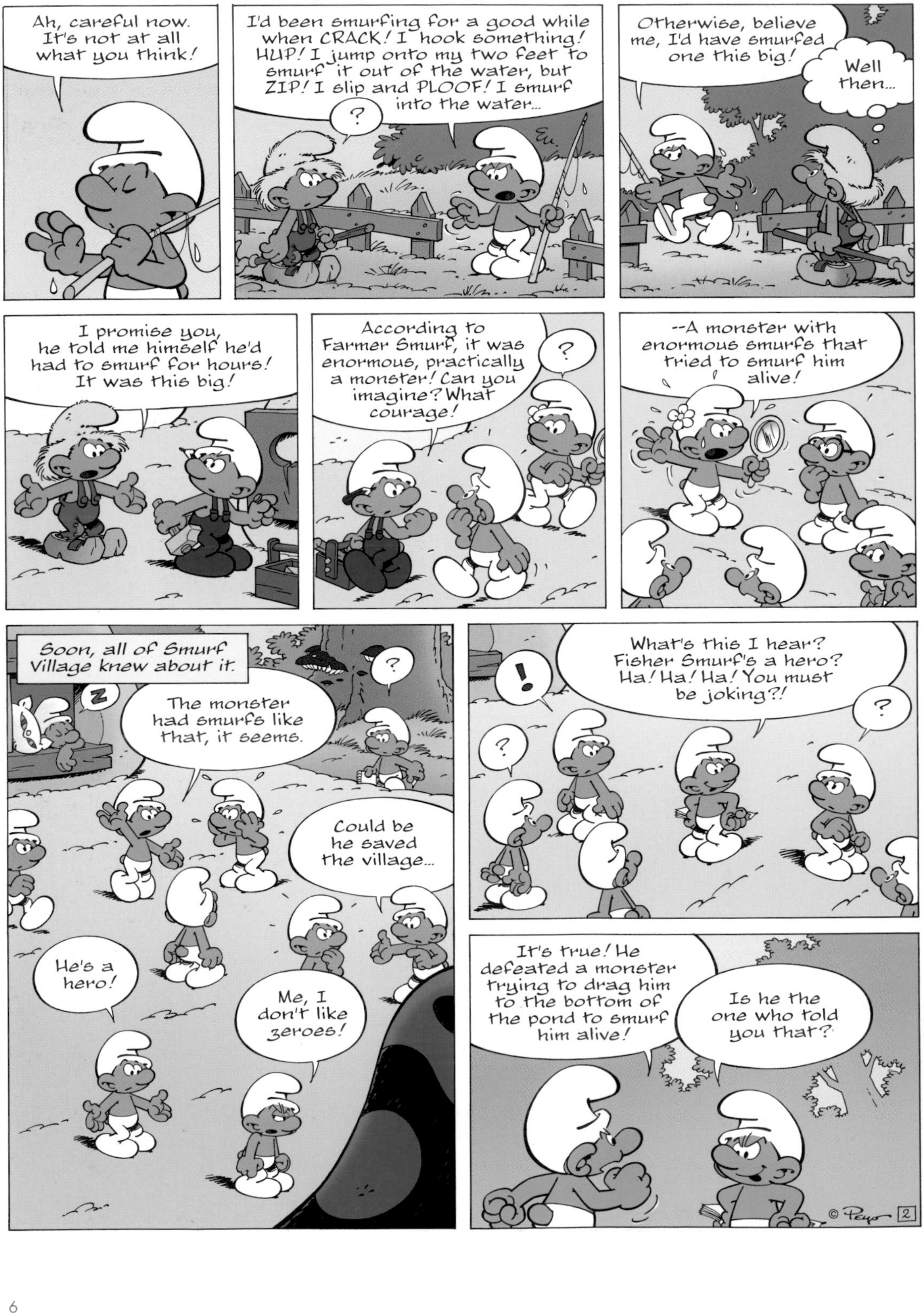

Ah, careful now. It's not at all what you think!
I'd been smurfing for a good while when CRACK! I hook something! HUP! I jump onto my two feet to smurf it out of the water, but ZIP! I slip and PLOOF! I smurf into the water...
?
Otherwise, believe me, I'd have smurfed one this big!
Well then...
I promise you, he told me himself he'd had to smurf for hours! It was this big!
According to Farmer Smurf, it was enormous, practically a monster! Can you imagine? What courage!
?
--A monster with enormous smurfs that tried to smurf him alive!
Soon, all of Smurf Village knew about it.
Z
The monster had smurfs like that, it seems.
?
Could be he saved the village...
He's a hero!
Me, I don't like zeroes!
!
What's this I hear? Fisher Smurf's a hero? Ha! Ha! Ha! You must be joking?!
?
?
It's true! He defeated a monster trying to drag him to the bottom of the pond to smurf him alive!
Is he the one who told you that?
© Peyo 2

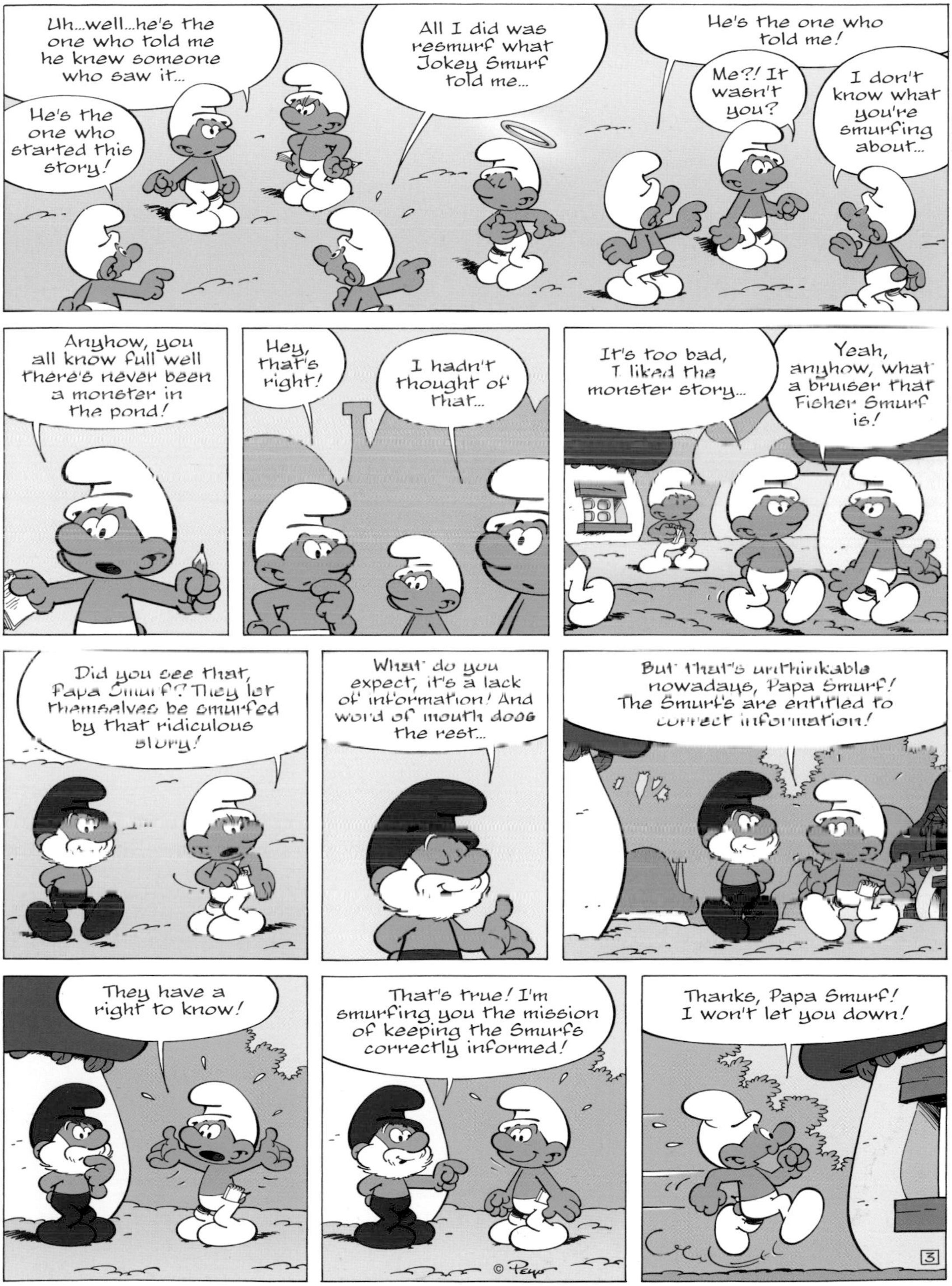
He's the one who started this story!
Uh...well...he's the one who told me he knew someone who saw it...
All I did was resmurf what Jokey Smurf told me...
He's the one who told me!
Me?! It wasn't you?
I don't know what you're smurfing about...
Anyhow, you all know full well there's never been a monster in the pond!
Hey, that's right!
I hadn't thought of that...
It's too bad, I liked the monster story...
Yeah, anyhow, what a bruiser that Fisher Smurf is!
Did you see that, Papa Smurf? They let themselves be smurfed by that ridiculous story!
What do you expect, it's a lack of information! And word of mouth does the rest...
But that's unthinkable nowadays, Papa Smurf! The Smurfs are entitled to correct information!
They have a right to know!
That's true! I'm smurfing you the mission of keeping the Smurfs correctly informed!
© Peyo
Thanks, Papa Smurf! I won't let you down!
3

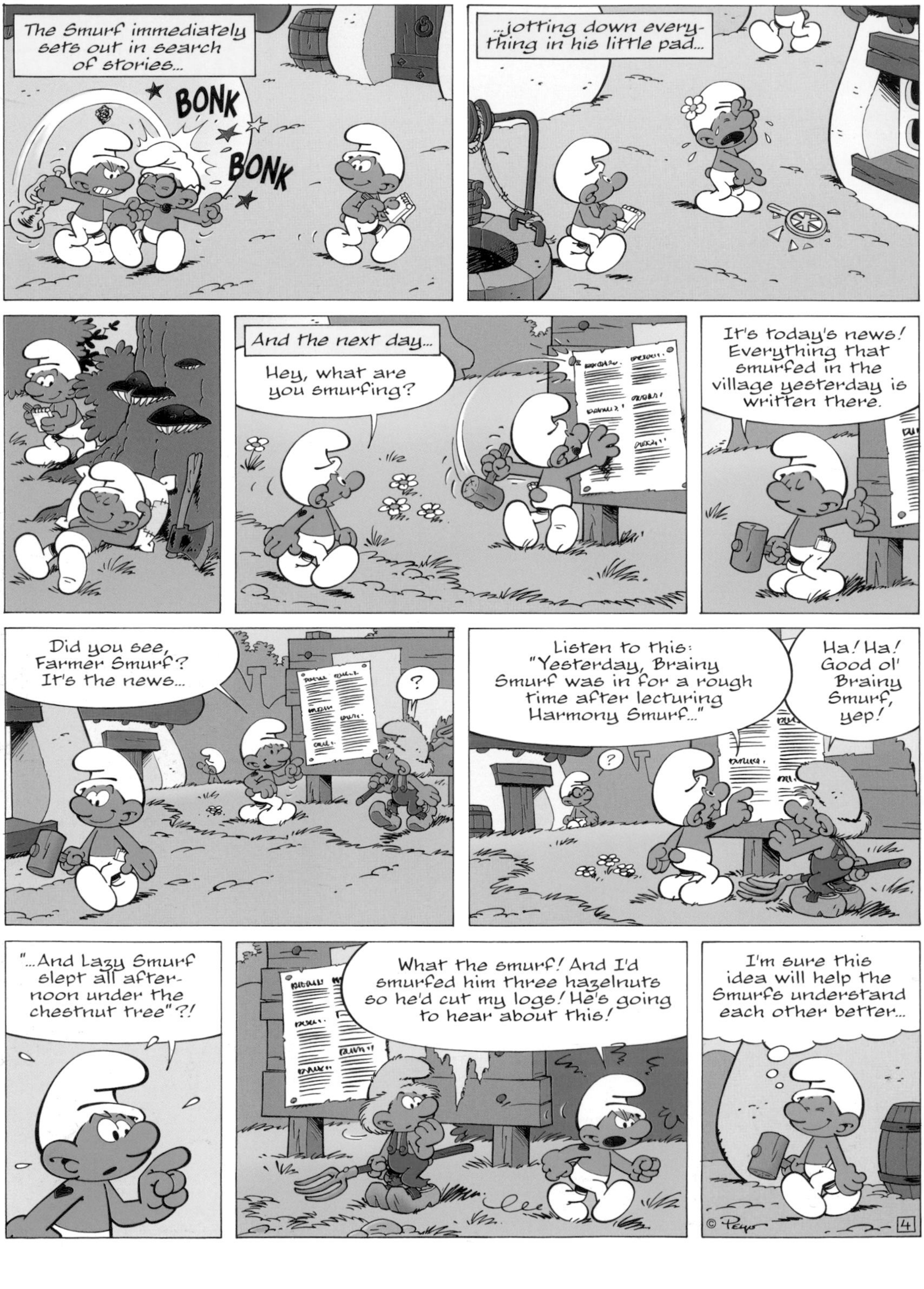
The Smurf immediately sets out in search of stories...
BONK
BONK
...jotting down everything in his little pad...
And the next day...
Hey, what are you smurfing?
It's today's news! Everything that smurfed in the village yesterday is written there.
Did you see, Farmer Smurf? It's the news...
?
Listen to this: "Yesterday, Brainy Smurf was in for a rough time after lecturing Harmony Smurf..."
Ha! Ha! Good ol' Brainy Smurf, yep!
?
"...And Lazy Smurf slept all afternoon under the chestnut tree"?!
What the smurf! And I'd smurfed him three hazelnuts so he'd cut my logs! He's going to hear about this!
I'm sure this idea will help the Smurfs understand each other better...
© Peyo
4

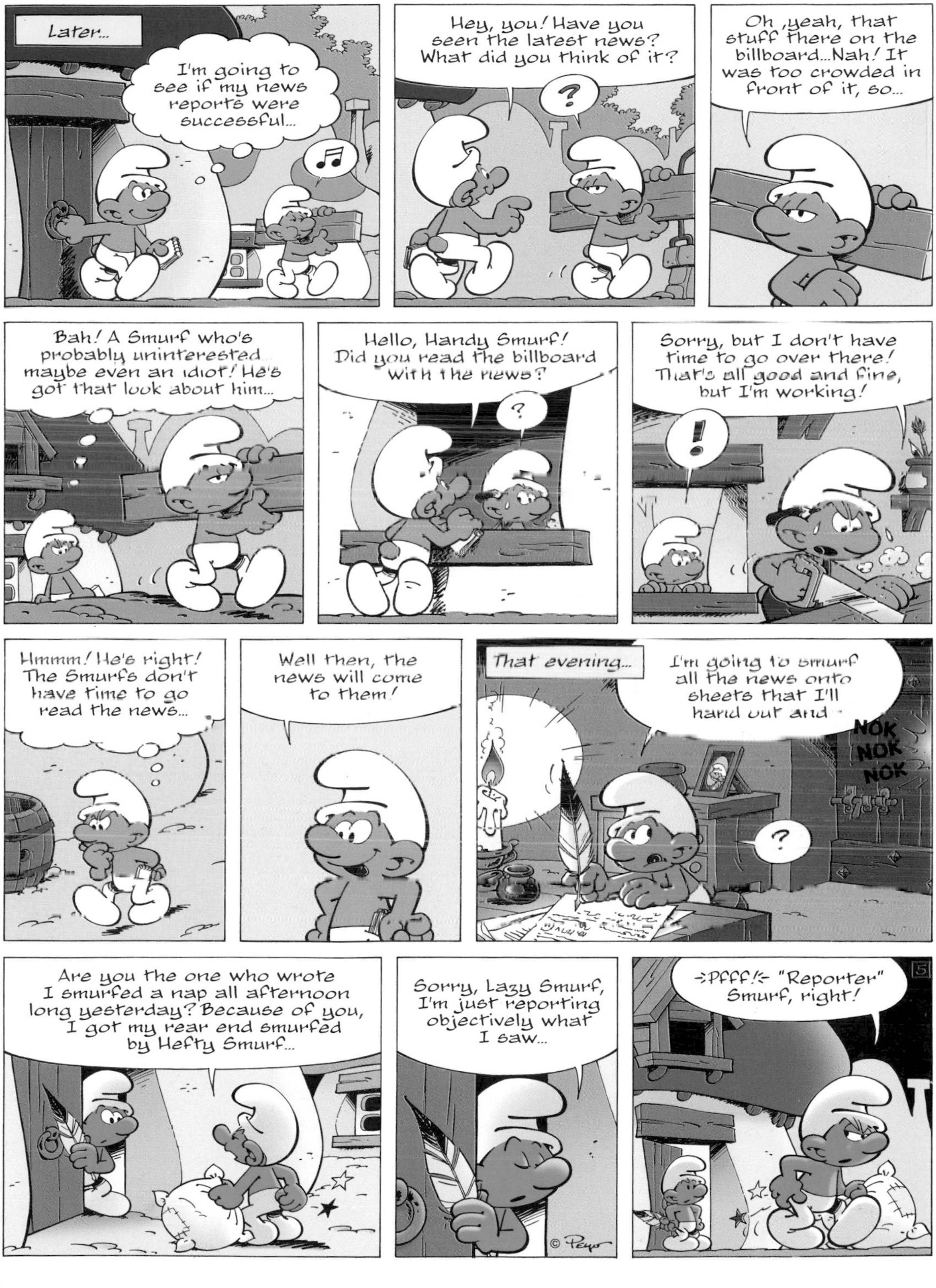

Later...
I'm going to see if my news reports were successful...
Hey, you! Have you seen the latest news? What did you think of it?
?
Oh ,yeah, that stuff there on the billboard...Nah! It was too crowded in front of it, so...
Bah! A Smurf who's probably uninterested maybe even an idiot! He's got that look about him...
Hello, Handy Smurf! Did you read the billboard with the news?
?
Sorry, but I don't have time to go over there! That's all good and fine, but I'm working!
!
Hmmm! He's right! The Smurfs don't have time to go read the news...
Well then, the news will come to them!
That evening...
I'm going to smurf all the news onto sheets that I'll hand out and -
NOK NOK NOK
?
Are you the one who wrote I smurfed a nap all afternoon long yesterday? Because of you, I got my rear end smurfed by Hefty Smurf...
Sorry, Lazy Smurf, I'm just reporting objectively what I saw...
© Peyo
-Pfff!- "Reporter" Smurf, right!

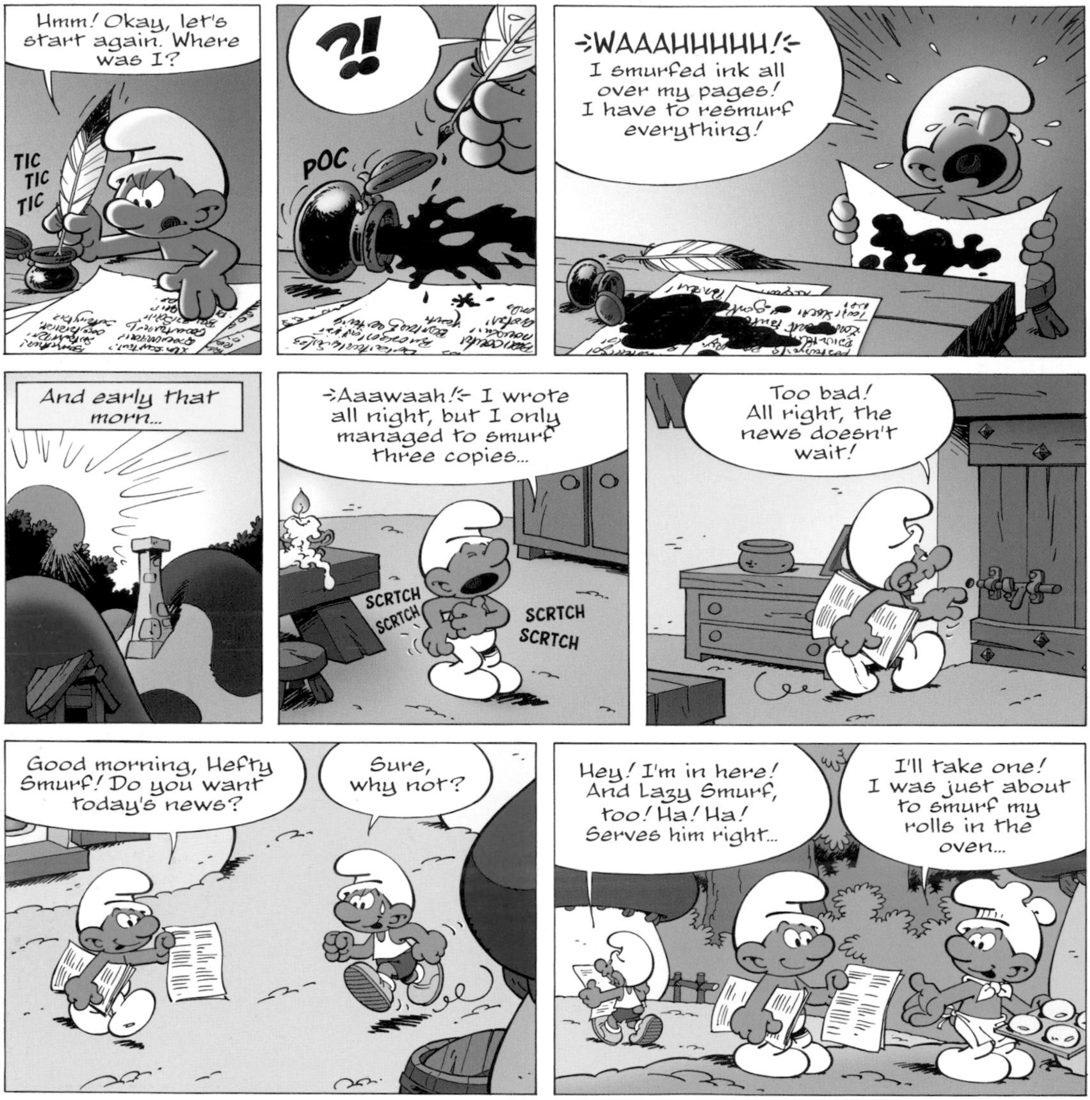

Hmm! Okay, let's start again. Where was I?
TIC TIC TIC
?!
POC
-WAAAHHHHH!- I smurfed ink all over my pages! I have to resmurf everything!
And early that morn...
-Aaawaah!- I wrote all night, but I only managed to smurf three copies...
SCRTCH SCRTCH
SCRTCH SCRTCH
Too bad! All right, the news doesn't wait!
Good morning, Hefty Smurf! Do you want today's news?
Sure, why not?
Hey! I'm in here! And Lazy Smurf, too! Ha! Ha! Serves him right...
I'll take one! I was just about to smurf my rolls in the oven...
WHO WANTS MY LAST COPY?!
ME!
I was first! I get to smurf it first!
No way! I asked for it first!
But...
© Peyo
6

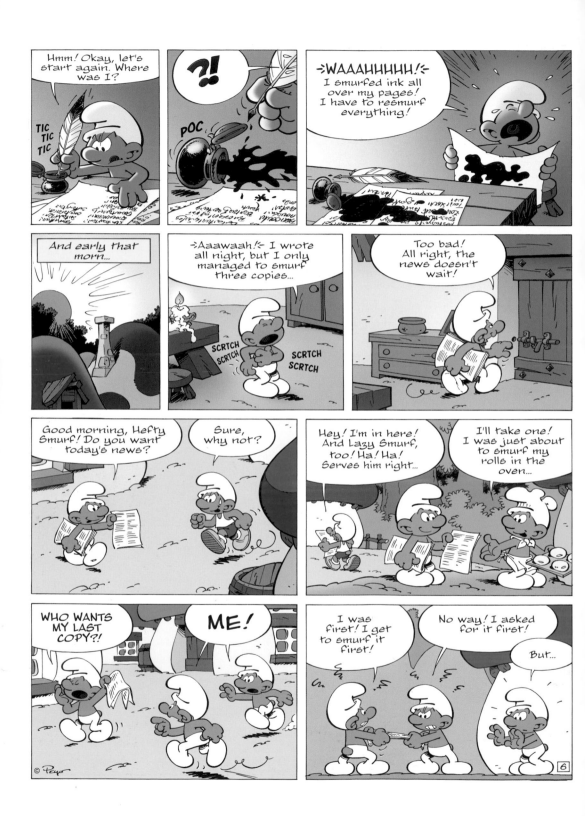

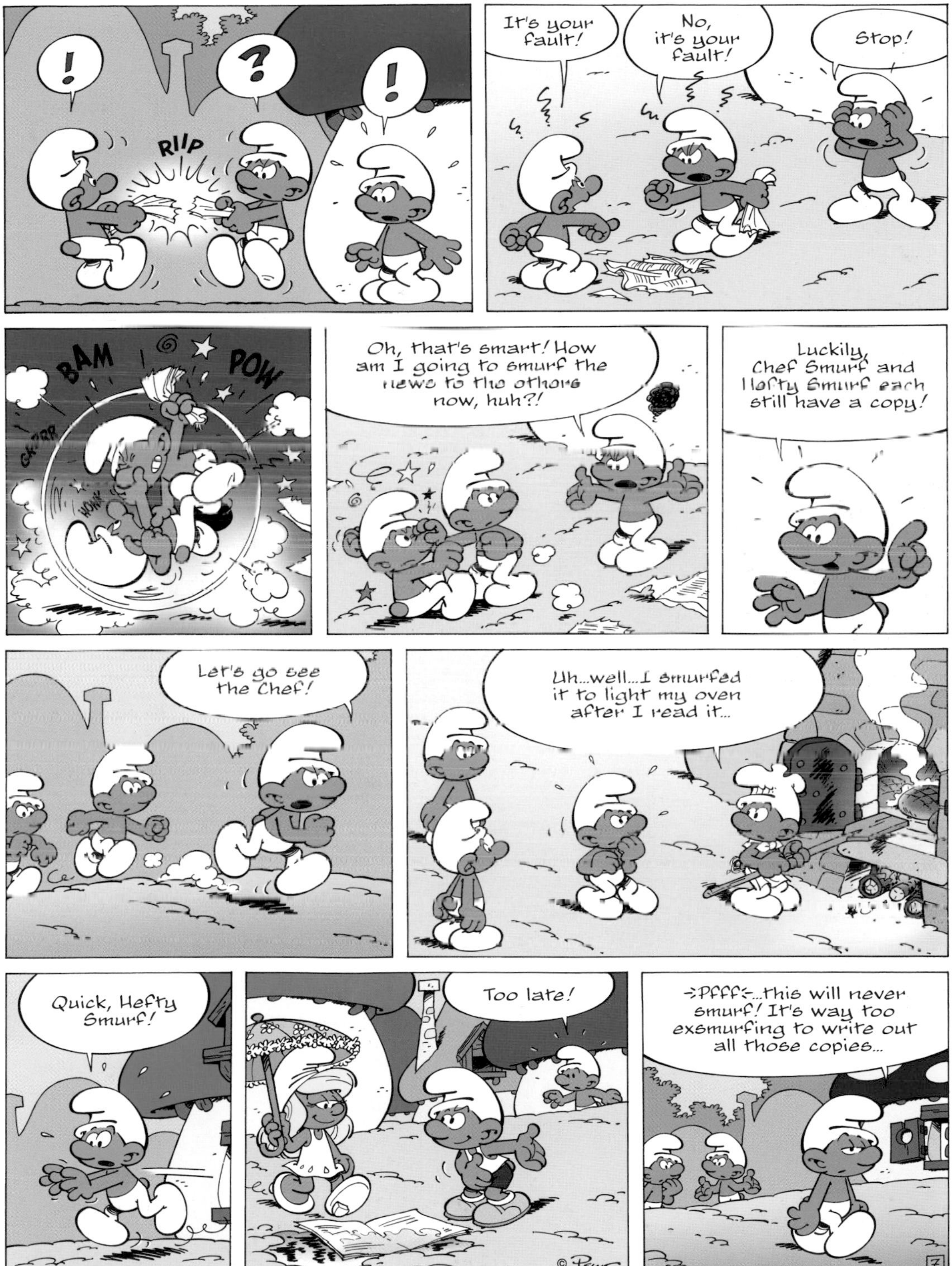
!
RIIP
?
!
It's your fault!
No, it's your fault!
Stop!
BAM
POW
Oh, that's smart! How am I going to smurf the news to the others now, huh?!
Luckily, Chef Smurf and Hefty Smurf each still have a copy!
Let's go see the Chef!
Uh...well...I smurfed it to light my oven after I read it...
Quick, Hefty Smurf!
Too late!
© Peyo
=Pfff=...this will never smurf! It's way too exsmurfing to write out all those copies...
7

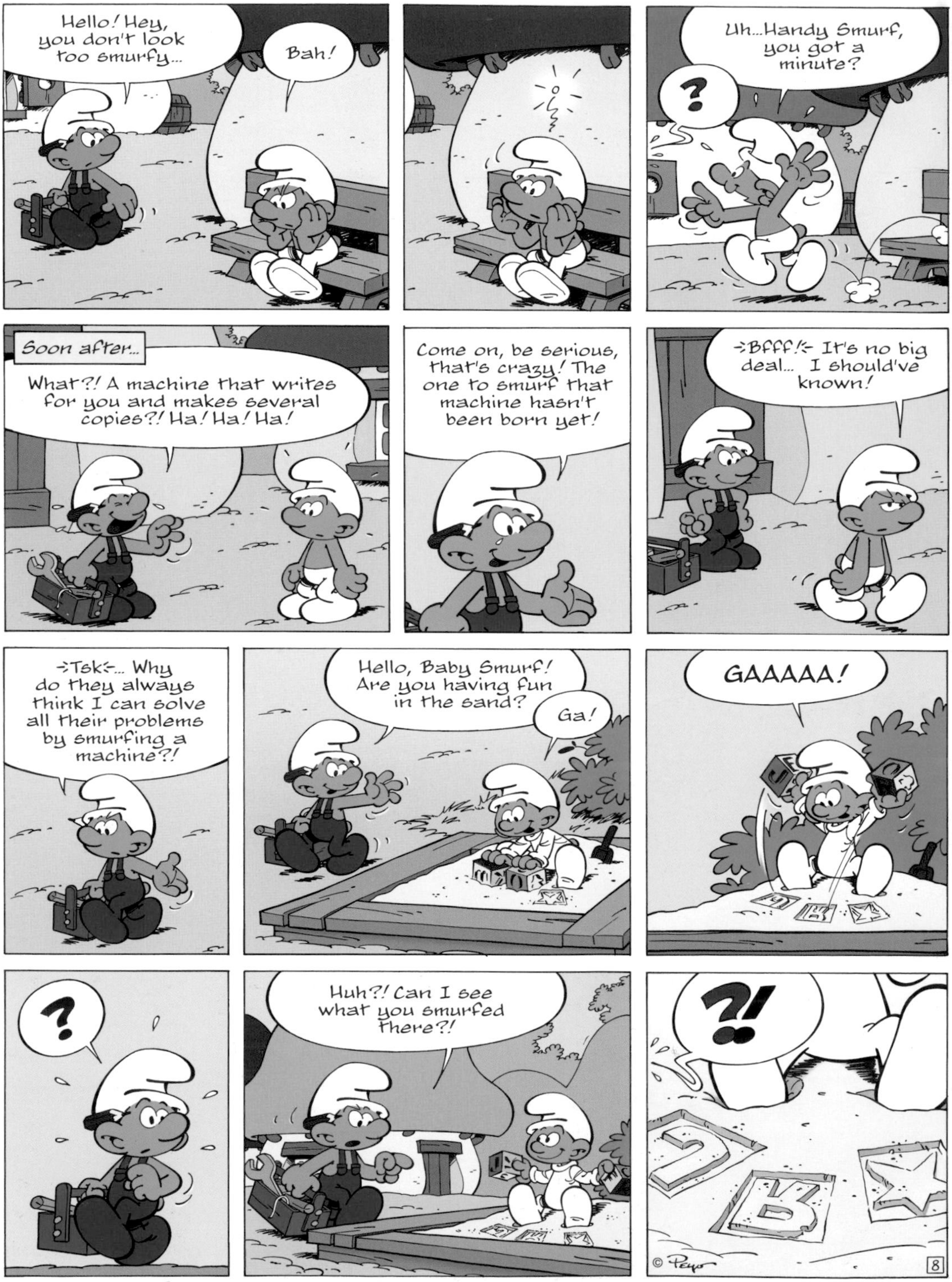
Hello! Hey, you don't look too smurfy...
Bah!
Uh... Handy Smurf, you got a minute?
?
Soon after...
What?! A machine that writes for you and makes several copies?! Ha! Ha! Ha!
Come on, be serious, that's crazy! The one to smurf that machine hasn't been born yet!
Bfff! It's no big deal... I should've known!
Tsk... Why do they always think I can solve all their problems by smurfing a machine?!
Hello, Baby Smurf! Are you having fun in the sand?
Ga!
GAAAAA!
?
Huh?! Can I see what you smurfed there?!
?!
© Peyo
8

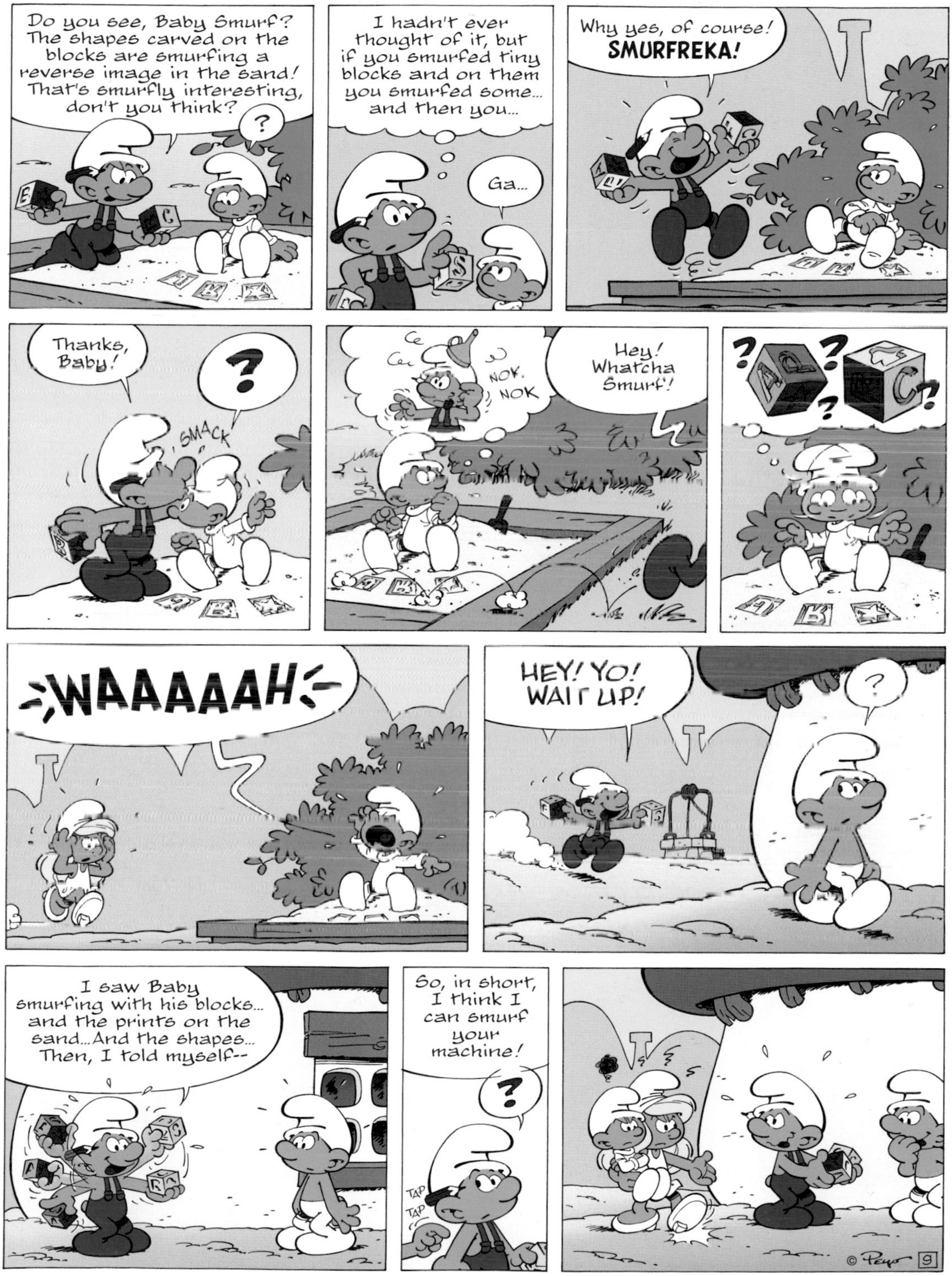

Do you see, Baby Smurf? The shapes carved on the blocks are smurfing a reverse image in the sand! That's smurfly interesting, don't you think?
?
I hadn't ever thought of it, but if you smurfed tiny blocks and on them you smurfed some... and then you...
Ga...
Why yes, of course! SMURFREKA!
Thanks, Baby!
?
SMACK
NOK NOK
Hey! Whatcha Smurf'!
WAAAAAH
HEY! YO! WAIT UP!
?
I saw Baby smurfing with his blocks... and the prints on the sand...And the shapes... Then, I told myself--
So, in short, I think I can smurf your machine!
?
TAP TAP
© Peyo 9

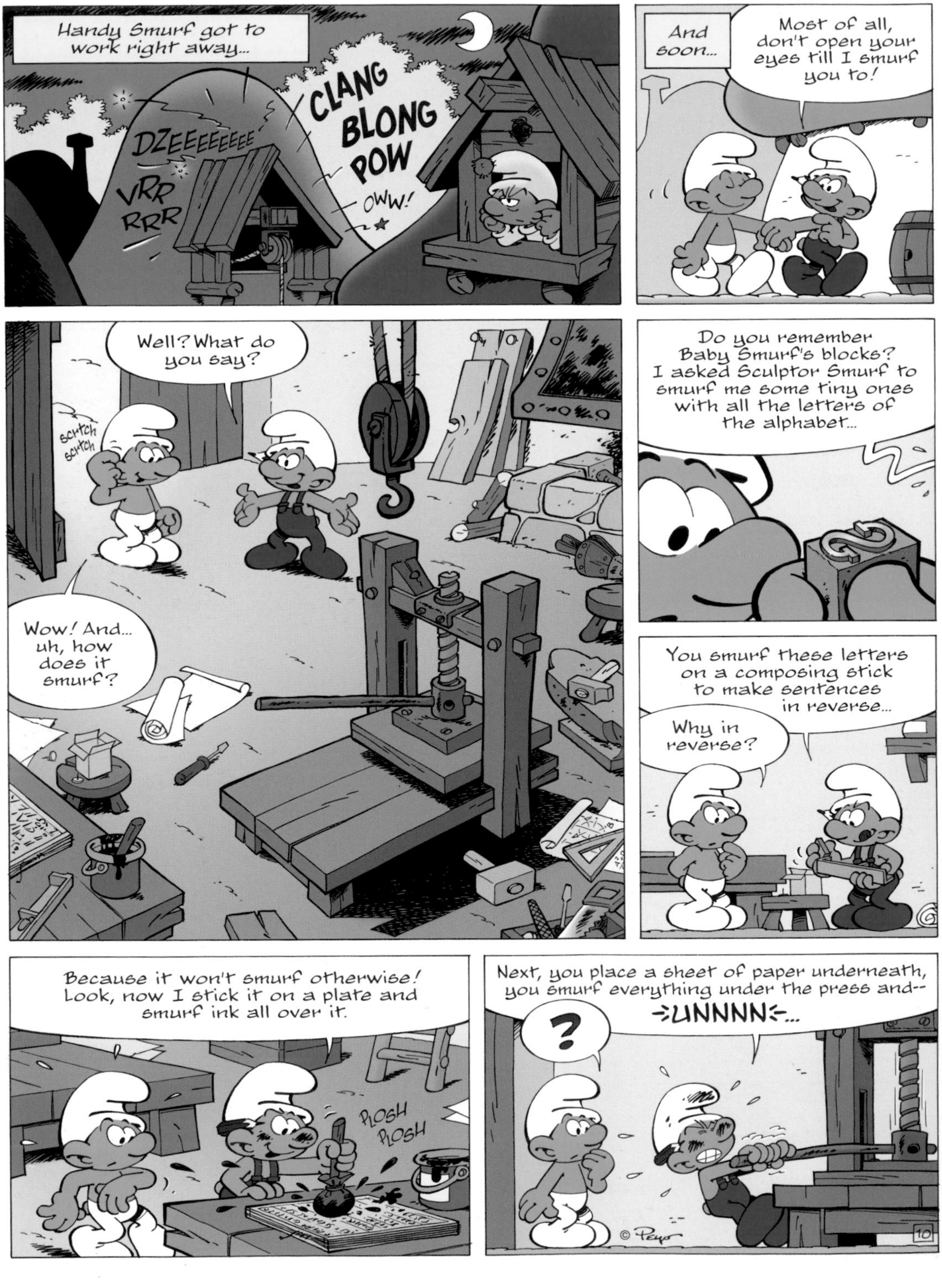
Handy Smurf got to work right away...
DZEEEEEEEE
VRR RRR
CLANG
BLONG
POW
OWW!
And soon...
Most of all, don't open your eyes till I smurf you to!
Well? What do you say?
scrtch scrtch
Wow! And... uh, how does it smurf?
Do you remember Baby Smurf's blocks? I asked Sculptor Smurf to smurf me some tiny ones with all the letters of the alphabet...
You smurf these letters on a composing stick to make sentences in reverse...
Why in reverse?
Because it won't smurf otherwise! Look, now I stick it on a plate and smurf ink all over it.
PLOSH PLOSH
Next, you place a sheet of paper underneath, you smurf everything under the press and--
UNNNN...
?
© Peyo
10

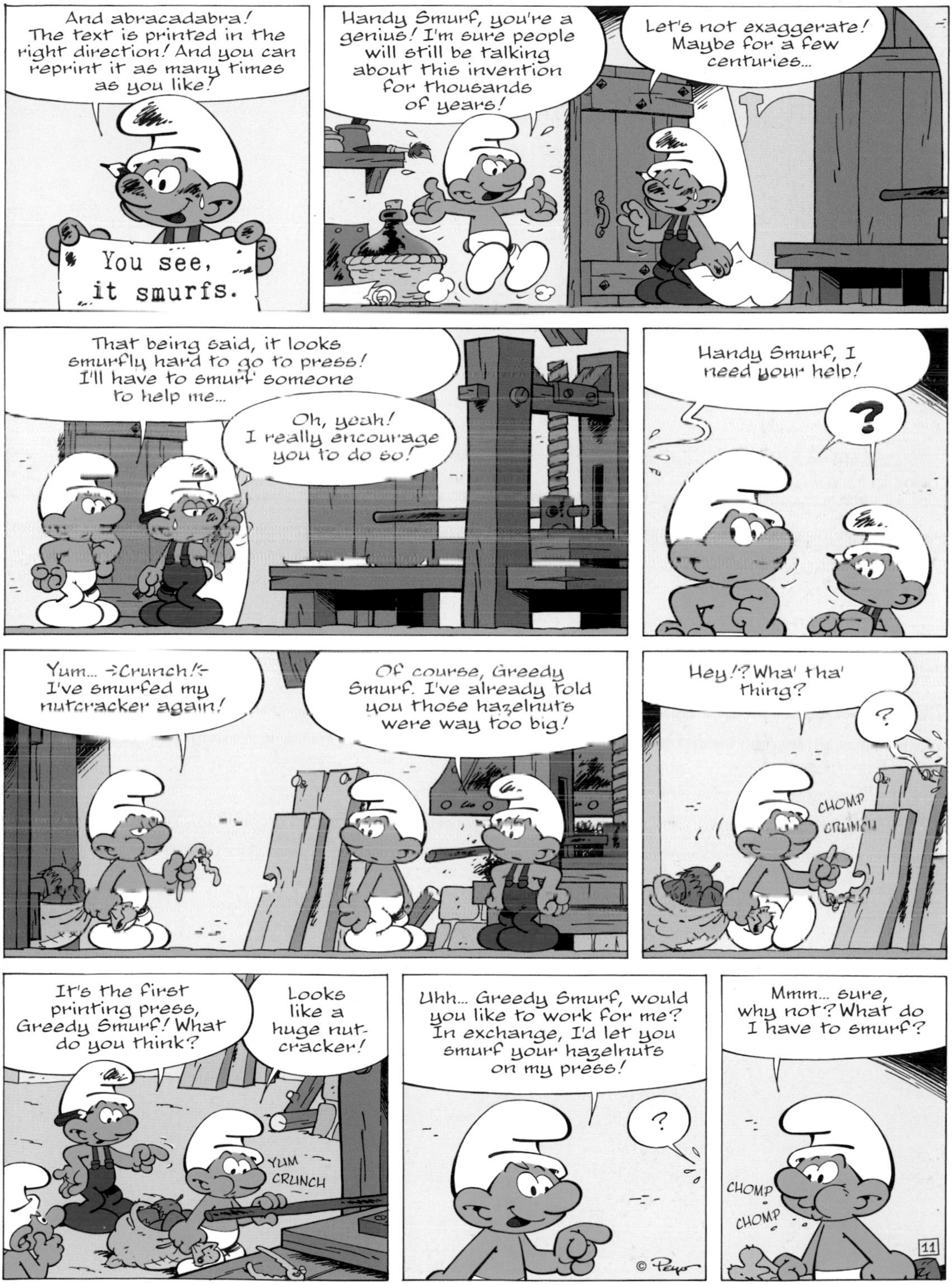
And abracadabra! The text is printed in the right direction! And you can reprint it as many times as you like!
You see, it smurfs.
Handy Smurf, you're a genius! I'm sure people will still be talking about this invention for thousands of years!
Let's not exaggerate! Maybe for a few centuries...
That being said, it looks smurfly hard to go to press! I'll have to smurf someone to help me...
Oh, yeah! I really encourage you to do so!
Handy Smurf, I need your help!
?
Yum... ⇝Crunch!⇜ I've smurfed my nutcracker again!
Of course, Greedy Smurf. I've already told you those hazelnuts were way too big!
Hey!? Wha' tha' thing?
?
CHOMP
CRUNCH
It's the first printing press, Greedy Smurf! What do you think?
Looks like a huge nut-cracker!
YUM
CRUNCH
Uhh... Greedy Smurf, would you like to work for me? In exchange, I'd let you smurf your hazelnuts on my press!
?
© Peyo
Mmm... sure, why not? What do I have to smurf?
CHOMP
CHOMP
11

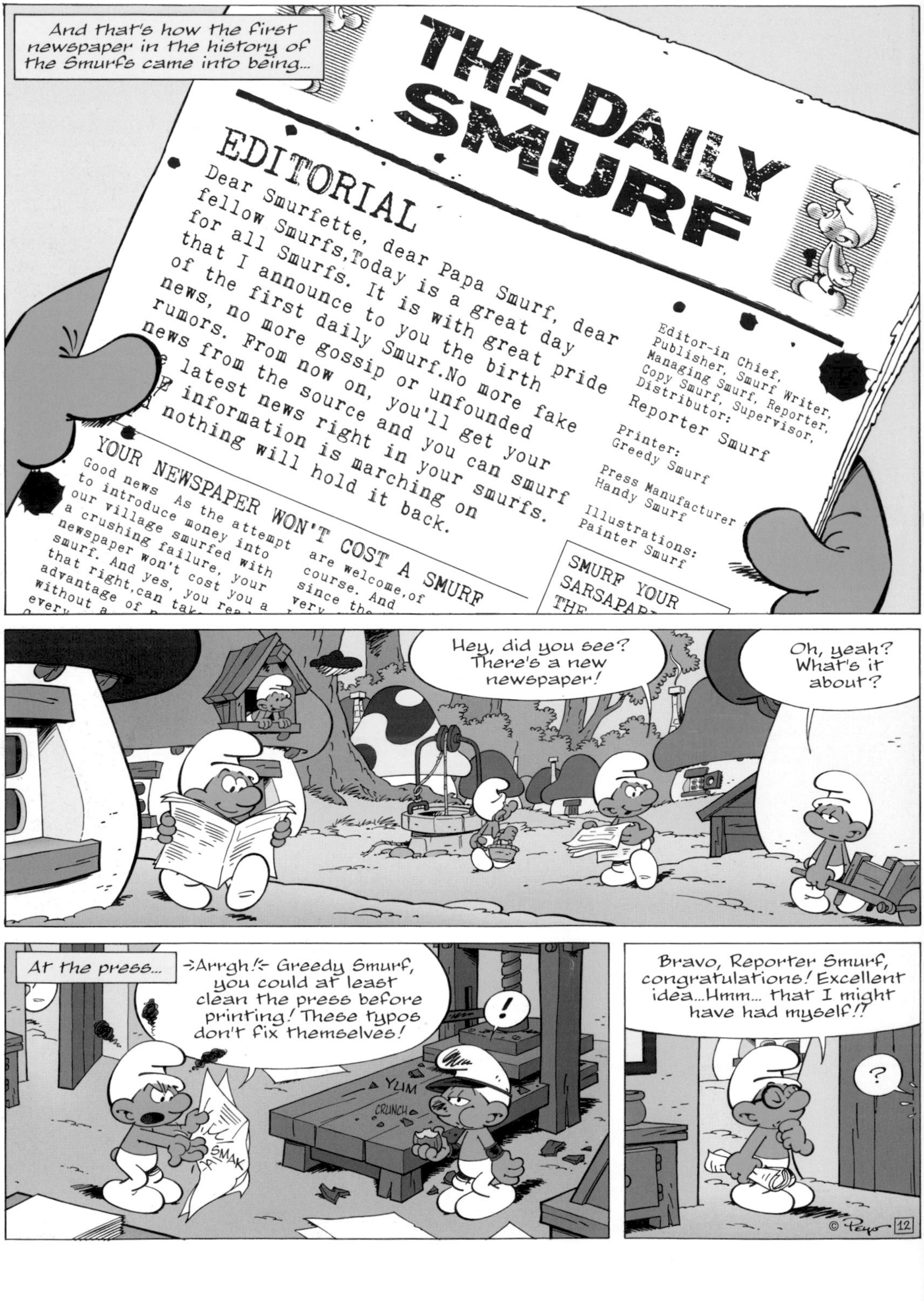

And that's how the first newspaper in the history of the Smurfs came into being...
THE DAILY SMURF
EDITORIAL
Dear Smurfette, dear Papa Smurf, dear fellow Smurfs,Today is a great day for all Smurfs. It is with great pride that I announce to you the birth of the first daily Smurf.No more fake news, no more gossip or unfounded rumors. From now on, you'll get your news from the source and you can smurf
latest news right in your smurfs.
information is marching on
nothing will hold it back.
Editor-in Chief, Publisher, Smurf Writer, Managing Smurf, Reporter, Copy Smurf, Supervisor, Distributor: Reporter Smurf
Printer: Greedy Smurf
Press Manufacturer Handy Smurf
Illustrations: Painter Smurf
YOUR NEWSPAPER WON'T COST A SMURF
Good news As the attempt to introduce money into our village smurfed with a crushing failure, your newspaper won't cost you a smurf. And yes, you read that right,can take
are welcome,of course. And
SMURF YOUR
Hey, did you see? There's a new newspaper!
Oh, yeah? What's it about?
At the press...
Arrgh! Greedy Smurf, you could at least clean the press before printing! These typos don't fix themselves!
!
YUM
CRUNCH
SMAK
Bravo, Reporter Smurf, congratulations! Excellent idea...Hmm... that I might have had myself!?
?
© Peyo 12

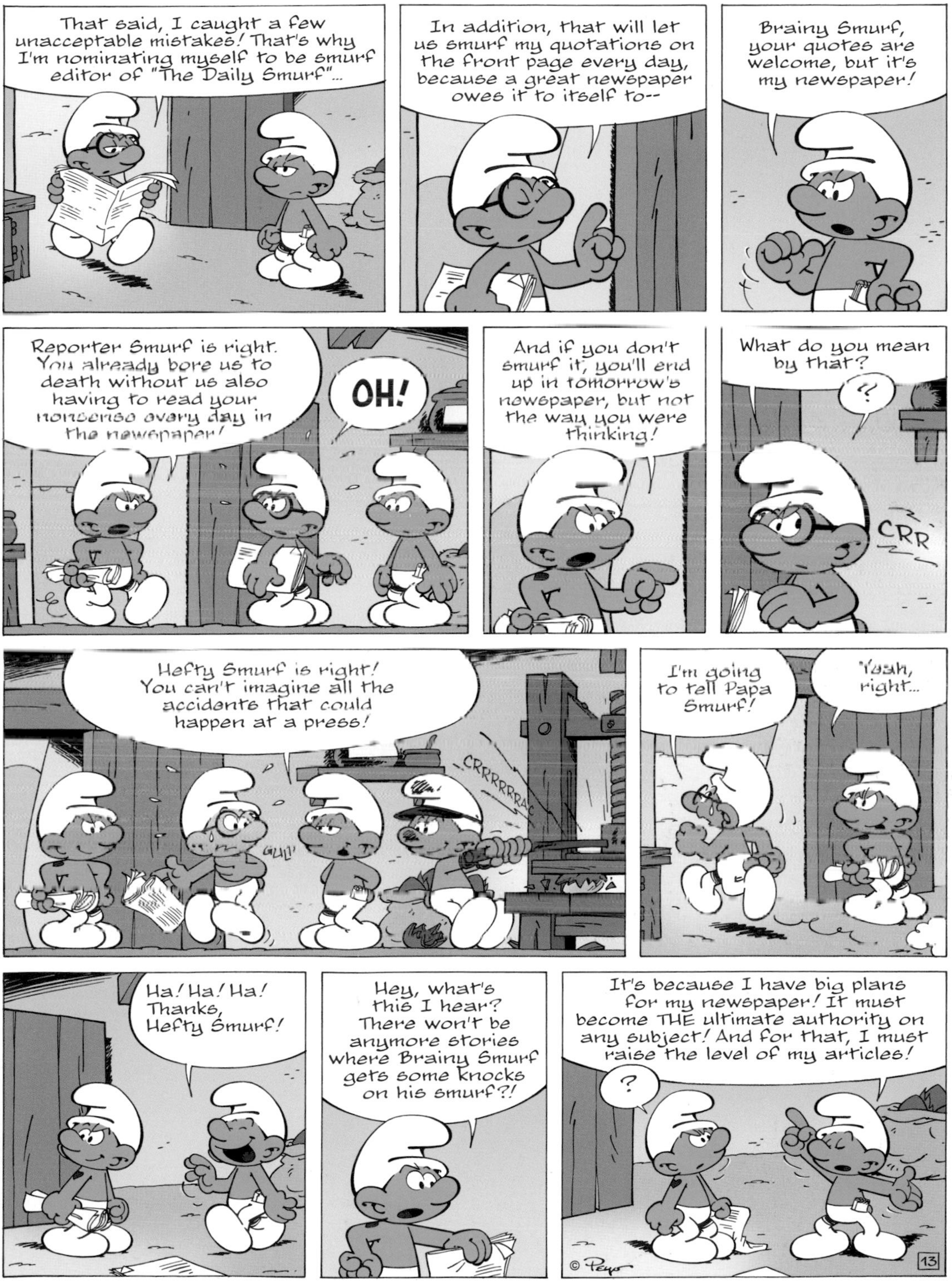
That said, I caught a few unacceptable mistakes! That's why I'm nominating myself to be smurf editor of "The Daily Smurf"...
In addition, that will let us smurf my quotations on the front page every day, because a great newspaper owes it to itself to--
Brainy Smurf, your quotes are welcome, but it's my newspaper!
Reporter Smurf is right. You already bore us to death without us also having to read your nonsense every day in the newspaper!
OH!
And if you don't smurf it, you'll end up in tomorrow's newspaper, but not the way you were thinking!
What do you mean by that?
??
CRR
Hefty Smurf is right! You can't imagine all the accidents that could happen at a press!
CRRRRRRAC
GULP
I'm going to tell Papa Smurf!
Yeah, right...
Ha! Ha! Ha! Thanks, Hefty Smurf!
Hey, what's this I hear? There won't be anymore stories where Brainy Smurf gets some knocks on his smurf?!
It's because I have big plans for my newspaper! It must become THE ultimate authority on any subject! And for that, I must raise the level of my articles!
?
© Peyo
13

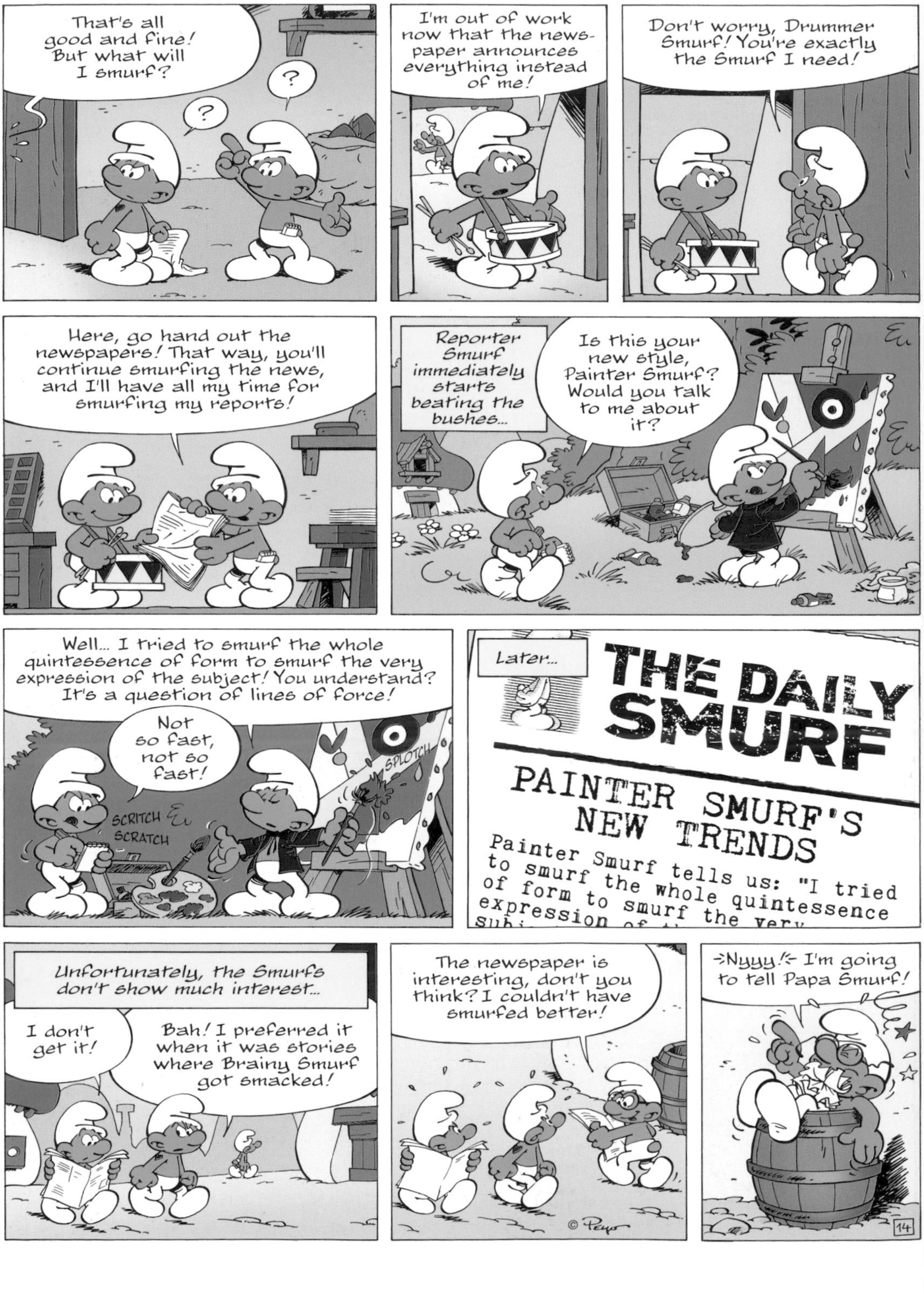
That's all good and fine! But what will I smurf?
?
?
I'm out of work now that the news-paper announces everything instead of me!
Don't worry, Drummer Smurf! You're exactly the Smurf I need!
Here, go hand out the newspapers! That way, you'll continue smurfing the news, and I'll have all my time for smurfing my reports!
Reporter Smurf immediately starts beating the bushes...
Is this your new style, Painter Smurf? Would you talk to me about it?
Well... I tried to smurf the whole quintessence of form to smurf the very expression of the subject! You understand? It's a question of lines of force!
Not so fast, not so fast!
SCRITCH SCRATCH
SPLOTCH
Later...
THE DAILY SMURF
PAINTER SMURF'S NEW TRENDS
Painter Smurf tells us: "I tried to smurf the whole quintessence of form to smurf the very expression of the
Unfortunately, the Smurfs don't show much interest...
I don't get it!
Bah! I preferred it when it was stories where Brainy Smurf got smacked!
The newspaper is interesting, don't you think? I couldn't have smurfed better!
© Peyo
-Nyyy!- I'm going to tell Papa Smurf!
14

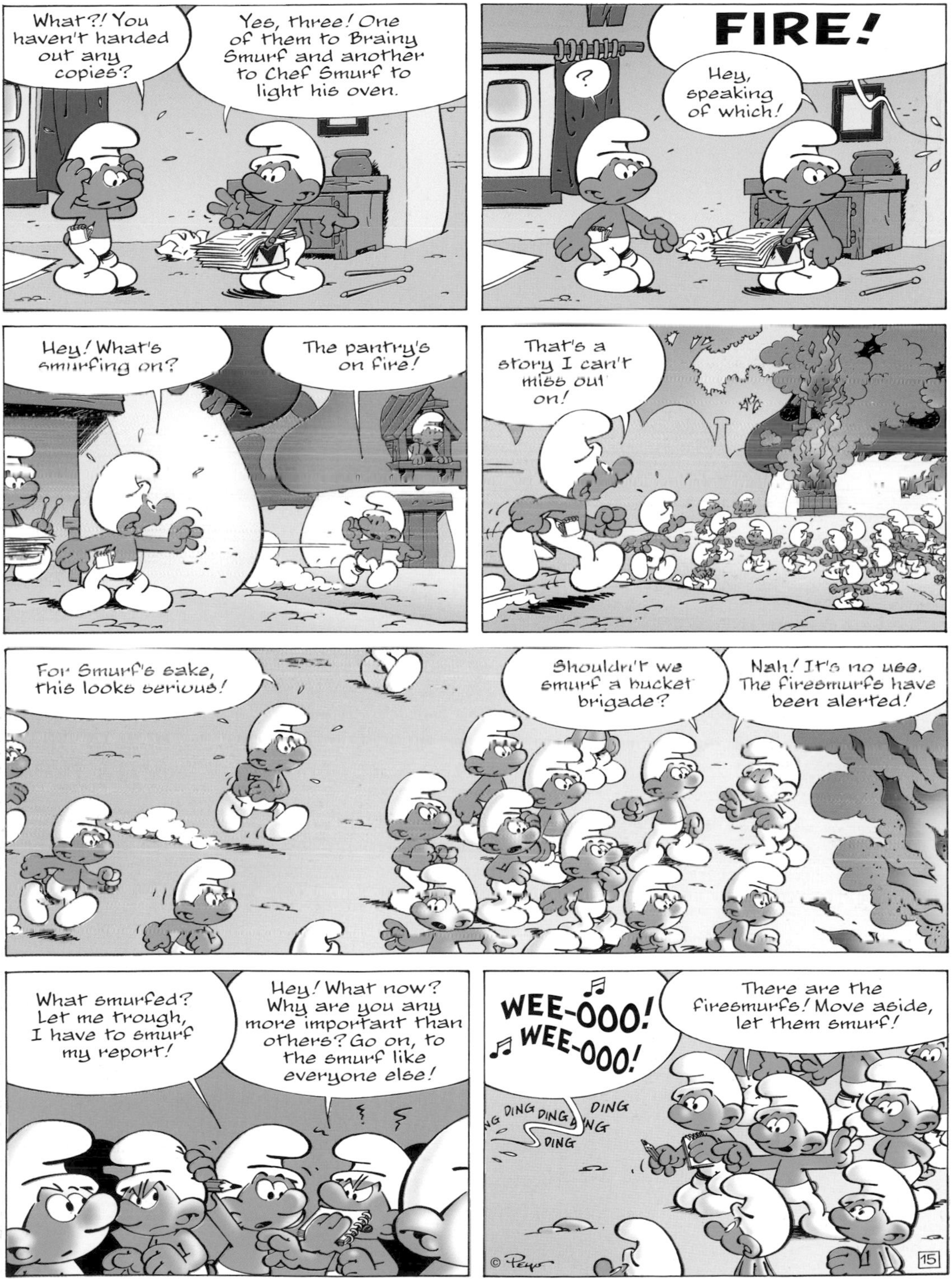
What?! You haven't handed out any copies?
Yes, three! One of them to Brainy Smurf and another to Chef Smurf to light his oven.
FIRE!
?
Hey, speaking of which!
Hey! What's smurfing on?
The pantry's on fire!
That's a story I can't miss out on!
For Smurf's sake, this looks serious!
Shouldn't we smurf a bucket brigade?
Nah! It's no use. The firesmurfs have been alerted!
What smurfed? Let me trough, I have to smurf my report!
Hey! What now? Why are you any more important than others? Go on, to the smurf like everyone else!
WEE-OOO! WEE-OOO!
DING DING DING DING DING
There are the firesmurfs! Move aside, let them smurf!
© Peyo
15

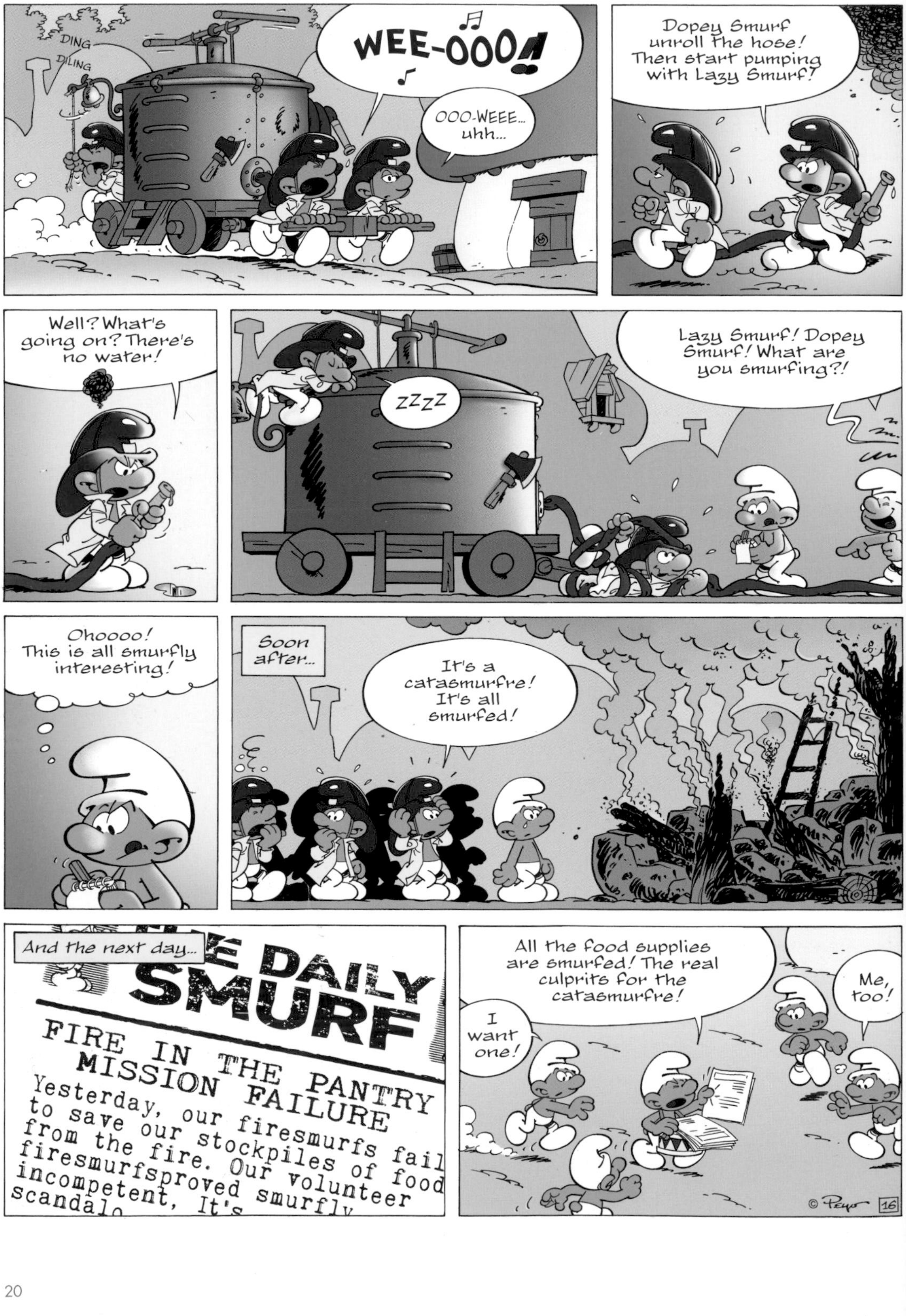
DING
DILING
WEE-OOO!
OOO-WEEE... uhh...
Dopey Smurf unroll the hose! Then start pumping with Lazy Smurf!
Well? What's going on? There's no water!
ZZZZ
Lazy Smurf! Dopey Smurf! What are you smurfing?!
Ohoooo! This is all smurfly interesting!
Soon after...
It's a catasmurfre! It's all smurfed!
And the next day...
THE DAILY SMURF
FIRE IN THE PANTRY
MISSION FAILURE
Yesterday, our firesmurfs fail to save our stockpiles of food from the fire. Our volunteer firesmurfsproved incompetent, It's smurfly scandalo
All the food supplies are smurfed! The real culprits for the catasmurfre!
I want one!
Me, too!
© Peyo
16

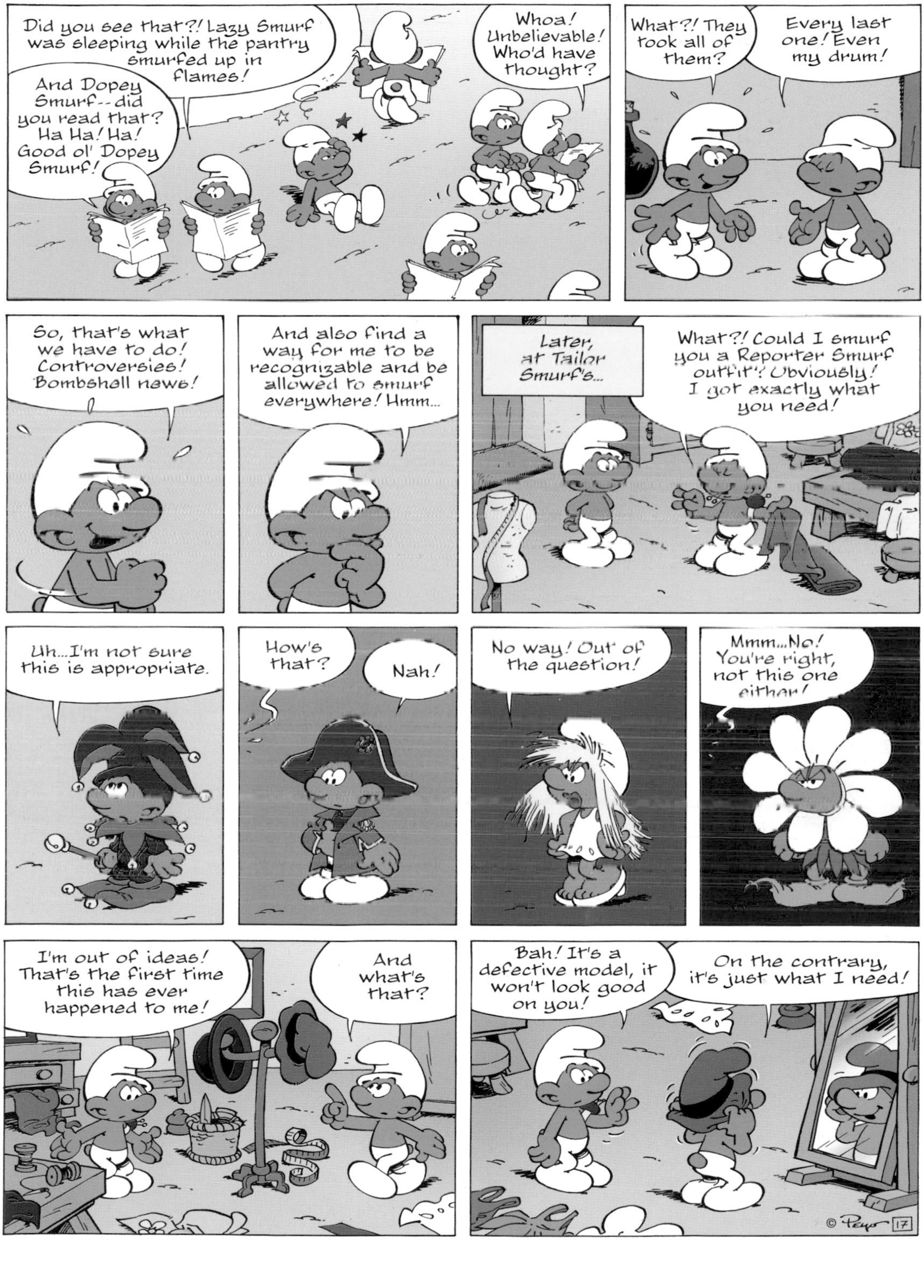
Did you see that?! Lazy Smurf was sleeping while the pantry smurfed up in flames!
And Dopey Smurf--did you read that? Ha Ha! Ha! Good ol' Dopey Smurf!
Whoa! Unbelievable! Who'd have thought?
What?! They took all of them?
Every last one! Even my drum!
So, that's what we have to do! Controversies! Bombshell news!
And also find a way for me to be recognizable and be allowed to smurf everywhere! Hmm...
Later, at Tailor Smurf's...
What?! Could I smurf you a Reporter Smurf outfit? Obviously! I got exactly what you need!
Uh...I'm not sure this is appropriate.
How's that?
Nah!
No way! Out of the question!
Mmm...No! You're right, not this one either!
I'm out of ideas! That's the first time this has ever happened to me!
And what's that?
Bah! It's a defective model, it won't look good on you!
On the contrary, it's just what I need!
© Peyo
17

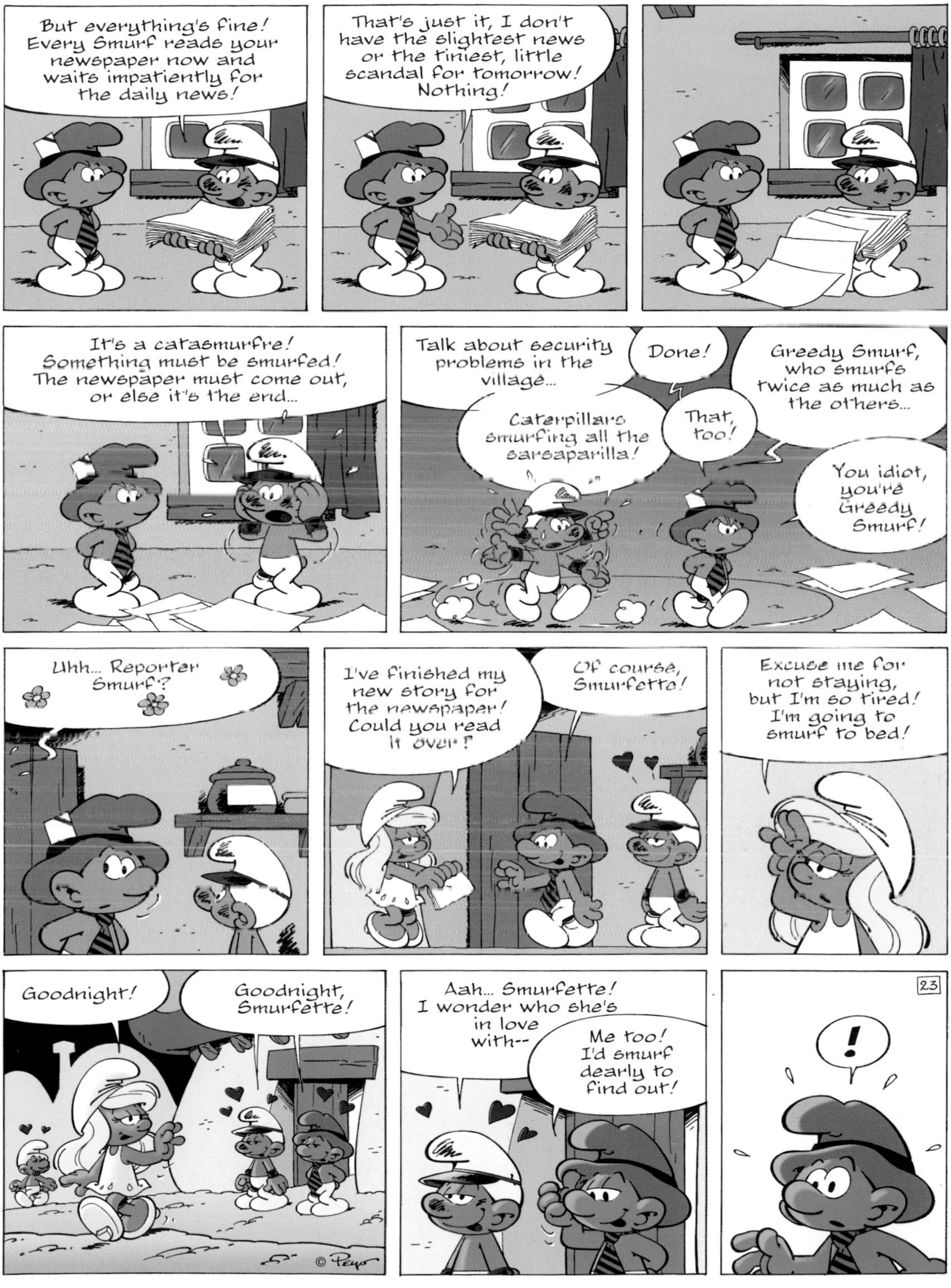

But everything's fine! Every Smurf reads your newspaper now and waits impatiently for the daily news!
That's just it, I don't have the slightest news or the tiniest, little scandal for tomorrow! Nothing!
It's a catasmurfre! Something must be smurfed! The newspaper must come out, or else it's the end...
Talk about security problems in the village...
Done!
Caterpillars smurfing all the sarsaparilla!
That, too!
Greedy Smurf, who smurfs twice as much as the others...
You idiot, you're Greedy Smurf!
Uhh... Reporter Smurf?
I've finished my new story for the newspaper! Could you read it over?
Of course, Smurfette!
Excuse me for not staying, but I'm so tired! I'm going to smurf to bed!
Goodnight!
Goodnight, Smurfette!
© Peyo
Aah... Smurfette! I wonder who she's in love with--
Me too! I'd smurf dearly to find out!
23
!

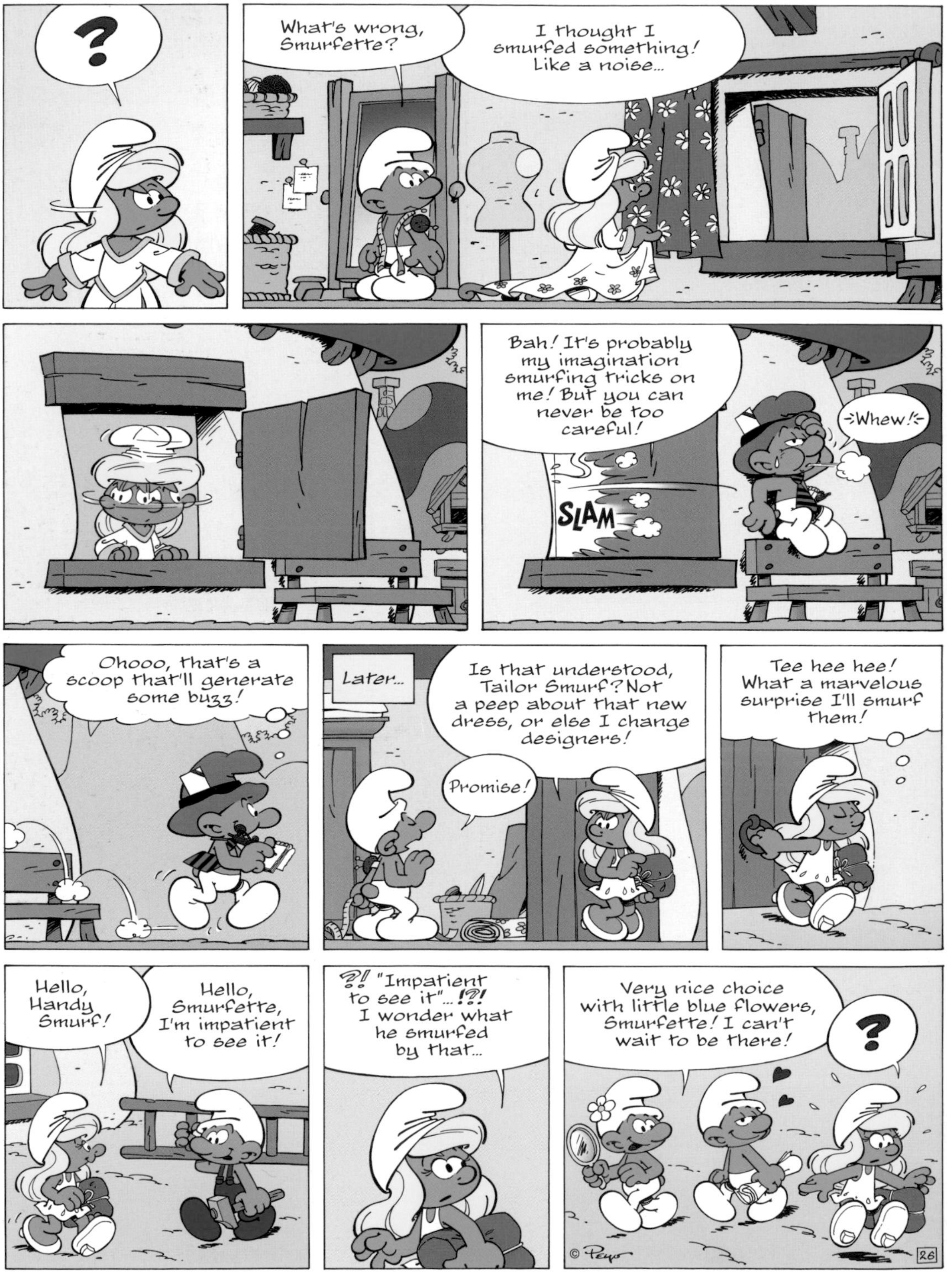
?
What's wrong, Smurfette?
I thought I smurfed something! Like a noise...
Bah! It's probably my imagination smurfing tricks on me! But you can never be too careful!
SLAM
Whew!
Ohooo, that's a scoop that'll generate some buzz!
Later...
Is that understood, Tailor Smurf? Not a peep about that new dress, or else I change designers!
Promise!
Tee hee hee! What a marvelous surprise I'll smurf them!
Hello, Handy Smurf!
Hello, Smurfette, I'm impatient to see it!
?! "Impatient to see it"...!?! I wonder what he smurfed by that...
Very nice choice with little blue flowers, Smurfette! I can't wait to be there!
?
© Peyo
26

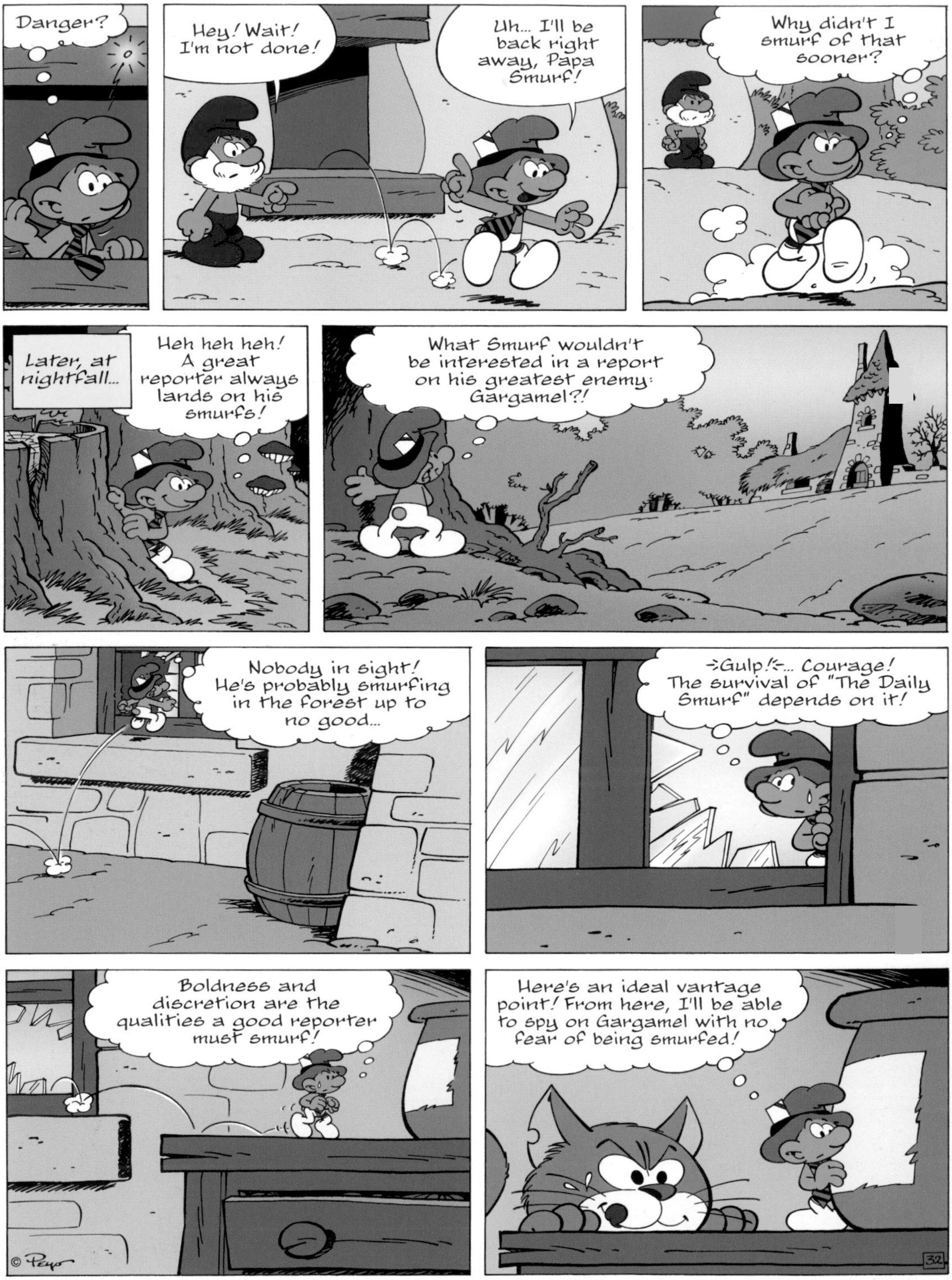

Danger?
Hey! Wait! I'm not done!
Uh... I'll be back right away, Papa Smurf!
Why didn't I smurf of that sooner?
Later, at nightfall...
Heh heh heh! A great reporter always lands on his smurfs!
What Smurf wouldn't be interested in a report on his greatest enemy: Gargamel?!
Nobody in sight! He's probably smurfing in the forest up to no good...
→Gulp!←... Courage! The survival of "The Daily Smurf" depends on it!
Boldness and discretion are the qualities a good reporter must smurf!
Here's an ideal vantage point! From here, I'll be able to spy on Gargamel with no fear of being smurfed!
© Peyo
32

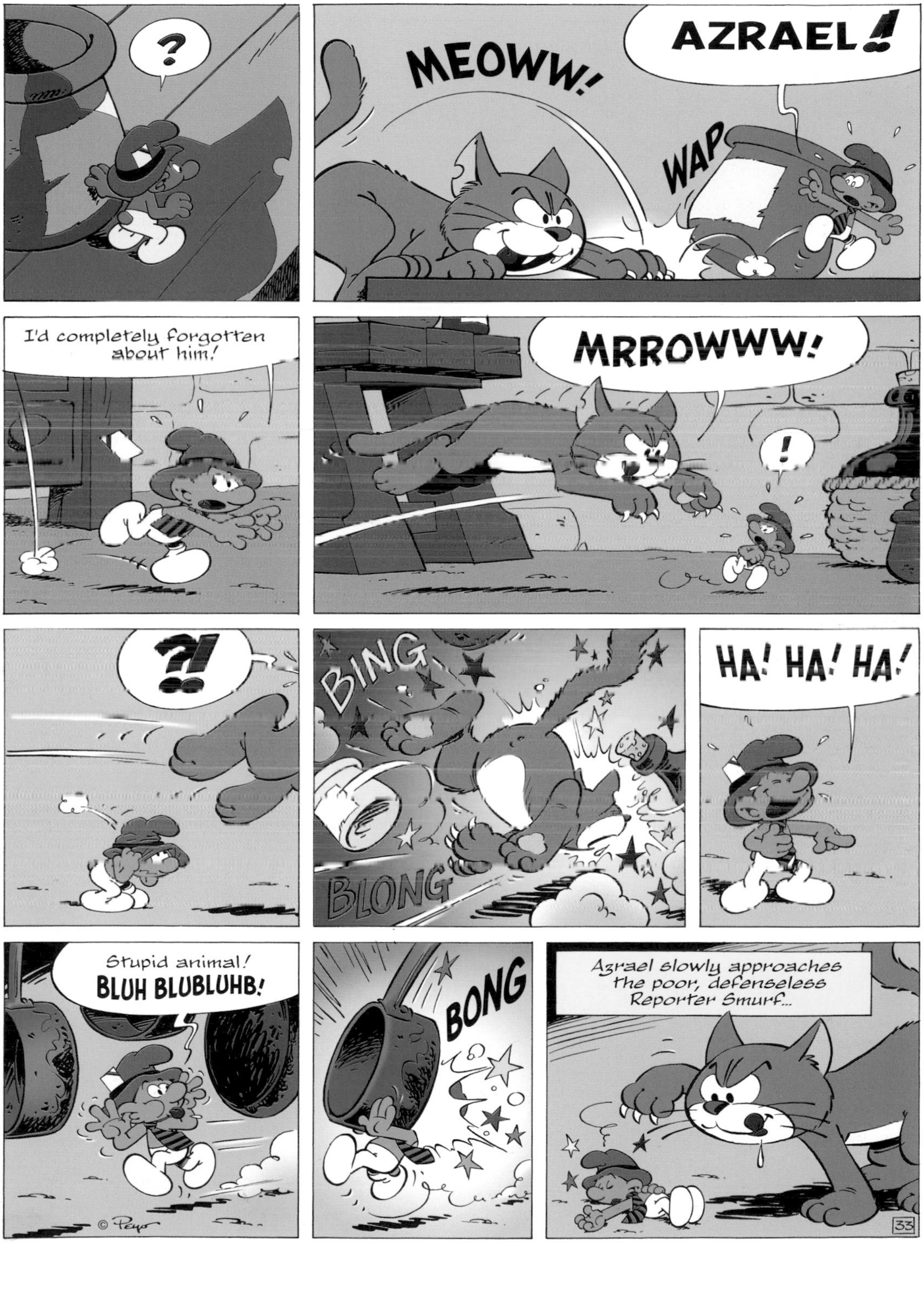
?
MEOWW!
AZRAEL!
WAP
I'd completely forgotten about him!
MRROWWW!
!
?!
BING
BLONG
HA! HA! HA!
Stupid animal!
BLUH BLUBLUHB!
© Peyo
BONG
Azrael slowly approaches the poor, defenseless Reporter Smurf...
33

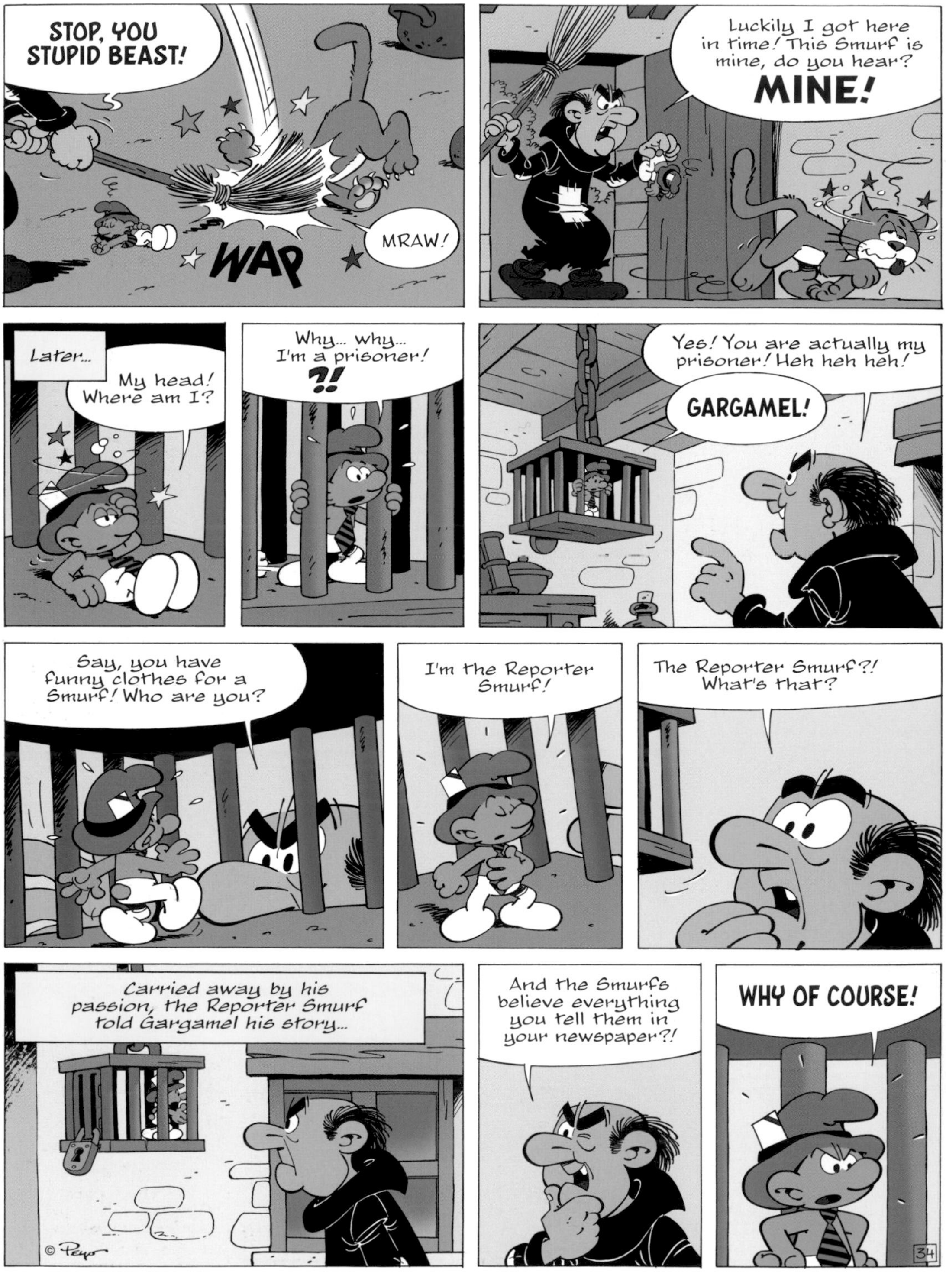
STOP, YOU STUPID BEAST!
WAP
MRAW!
Luckily I got here in time! This Smurf is mine, do you hear? MINE!
Later...
My head! Where am I?
Why... why... I'm a prisoner!
?!
Yes! You are actually my prisoner! Heh heh heh!
GARGAMEL!
Say, you have funny clothes for a Smurf! Who are you?
I'm the Reporter Smurf!
The Reporter Smurf?! What's that?
Carried away by his passion, the Reporter Smurf told Gargamel his story...
© Peyo
And the Smurfs believe everything you tell them in your newspaper?!
WHY OF COURSE!
34

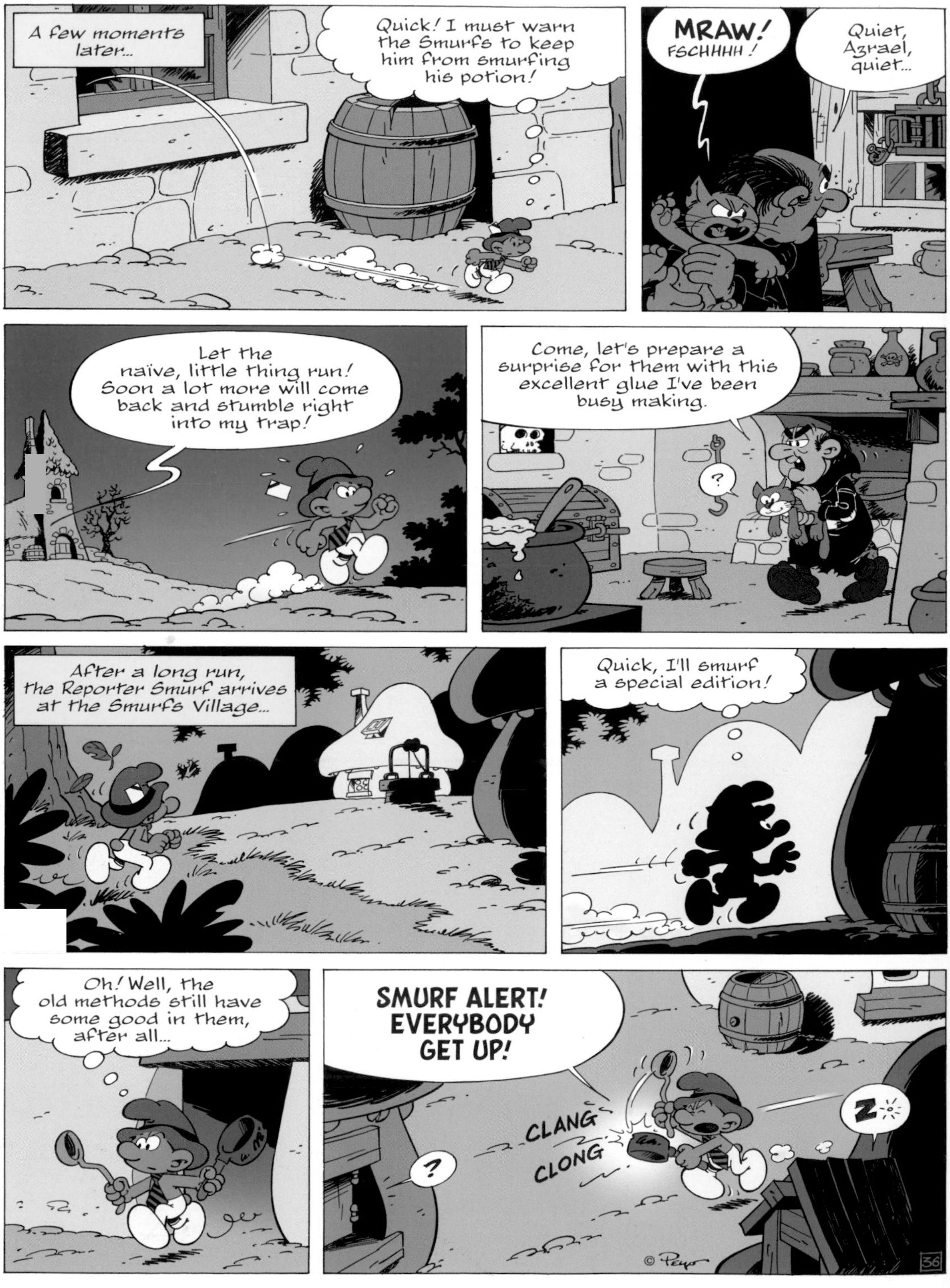
A few moments later...
Quick! I must warn the Smurfs to keep him from smurfing his potion!
MRAW! FSCHHHH!
Quiet, Azrael, quiet...
Let the naïve, little thing run! Soon a lot more will come back and stumble right into my trap!
Come, let's prepare a surprise for them with this excellent glue I've been busy making.
?
After a long run, the Reporter Smurf arrives at the Smurfs Village...
Quick, I'll smurf a special edition!
Oh! Well, the old methods still have some good in them, after all...
SMURF ALERT! EVERYBODY GET UP!
CLANG
CLONG
?
Z
© Peyo
36

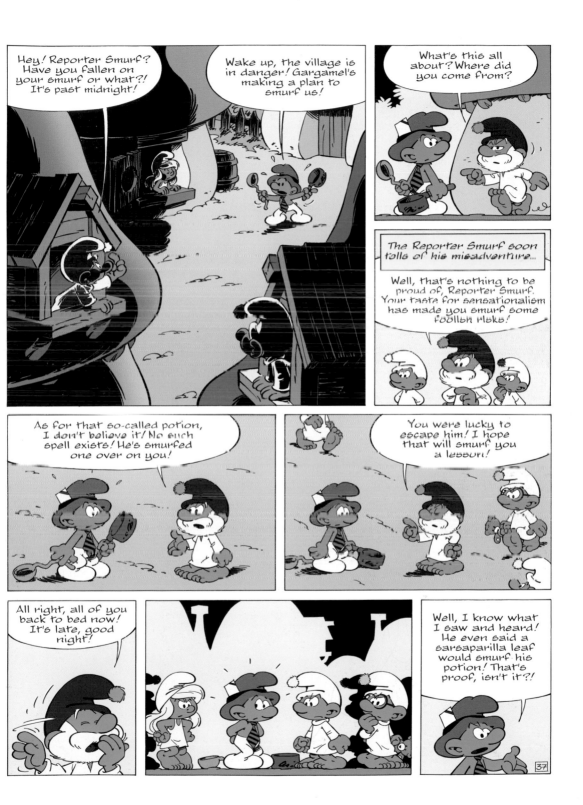

41

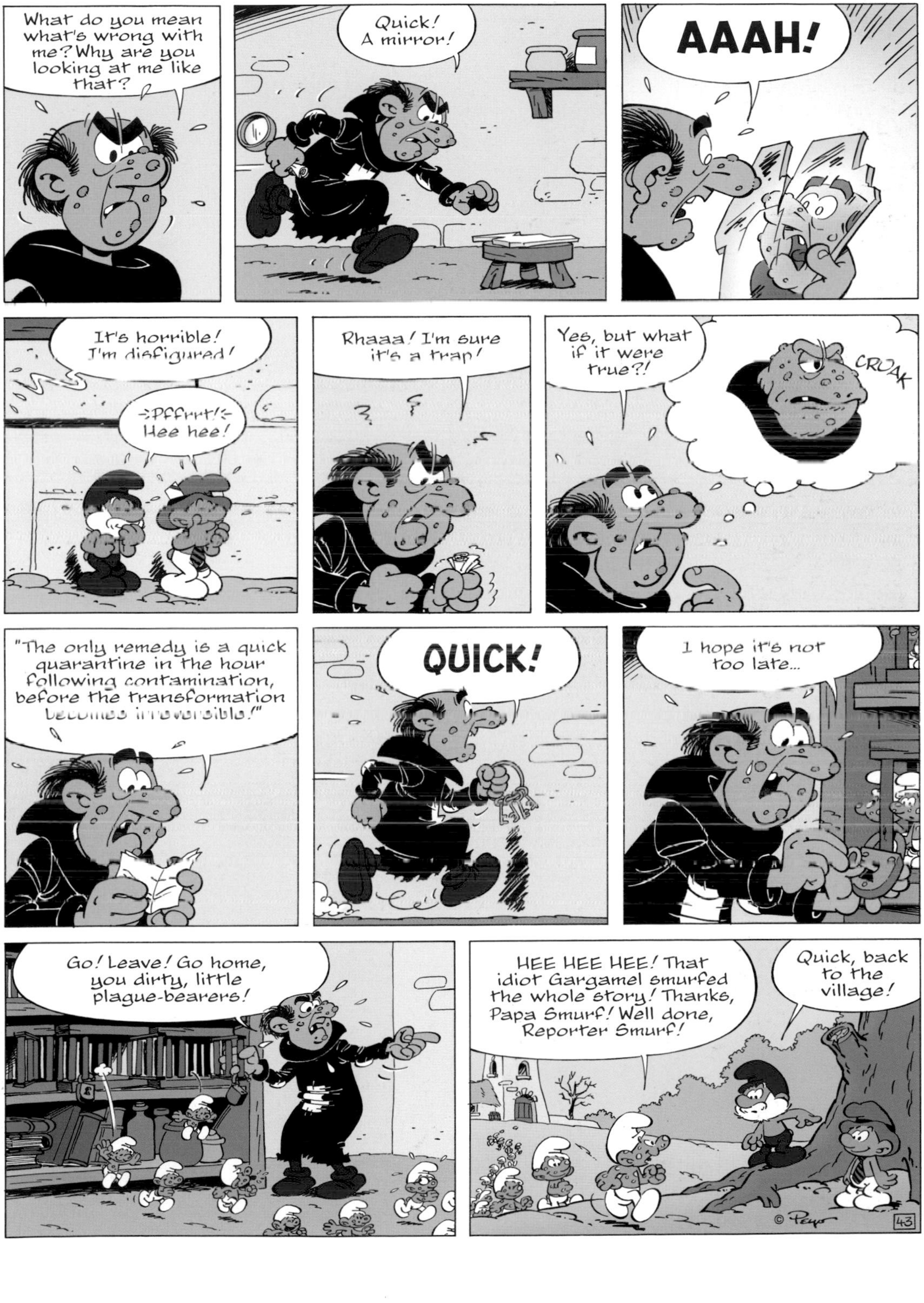

What do you mean what's wrong with me? Why are you looking at me like that?
Quick! A mirror!
AAAH!
It's horrible! I'm disfigured!
Pffrrt! Hee hee!
Rhaaa! I'm sure it's a trap!
Yes, but what if it were true?!
CROAK
"The only remedy is a quick quarantine in the hour following contamination, before the transformation becomes irreversible."
QUICK!
I hope it's not too late...
Go! Leave! Go home, you dirty, little plague-bearers!
HEE HEE HEE! That idiot Gargamel smurfed the whole story! Thanks, Papa Smurf! Well done, Reporter Smurf!
Quick, back to the village!
© Peyo
43

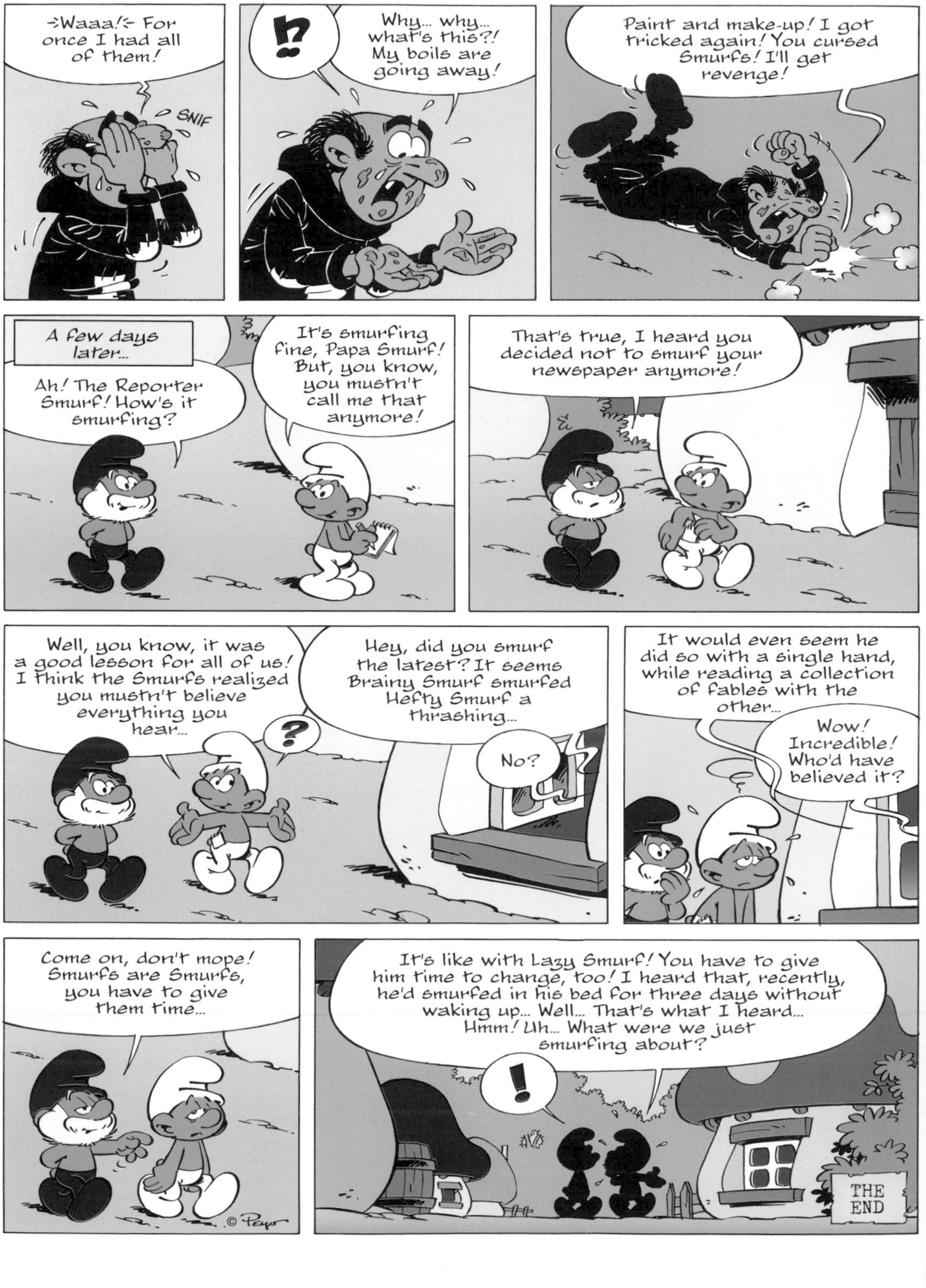

-Waaa!- For once I had all of them!
SNIF
?!
Why... why... what's this?! My boils are going away!
Paint and make-up! I got tricked again! You cursed Smurfs! I'll get revenge!
A few days later...
Ah! The Reporter Smurf! How's it smurfing?
It's smurfing fine, Papa Smurf! But, you know, you mustn't call me that anymore!
That's true, I heard you decided not to smurf your newspaper anymore!
Well, you know, it was a good lesson for all of us! I think the Smurfs realized you mustn't believe everything you hear...
?
Hey, did you smurf the latest? It seems Brainy Smurf smurfed Hefty Smurf a thrashing...
No?
It would even seem he did so with a single hand, while reading a collection of fables with the other...
Wow! Incredible! Who'd have believed it?
Come on, don't mope! Smurfs are Smurfs, you have to give them time...
© Peyo
It's like with Lazy Smurf! You have to give him time to change, too! I heard that, recently, he'd smurfed in his bed for three days without waking up... Well... That's what I heard... Hmm! Uh... What were we just smurfing about?
!
THE END

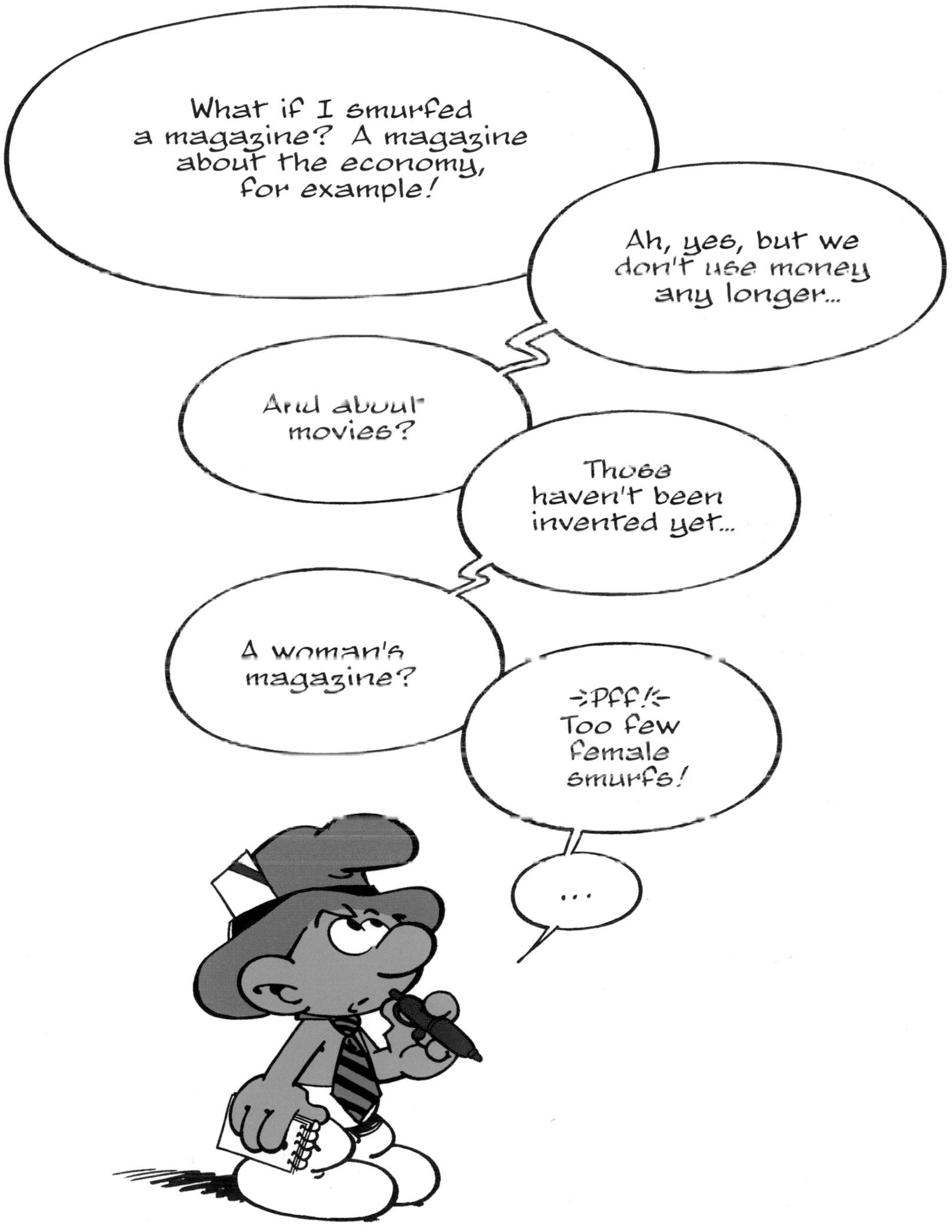
What if I smurfed a magazine? A magazine about the economy, for example!
Ah, yes, but we don't use money any longer...
And about movies?
Those haven't been invented yet...
A woman's magazine?
Pff! Too few female smurfs!
...

WATCH OUT FOR PAPERCUTZ™

Welcome to the totally-timely twenty-fourth SMURFS graphic novel by Peyo, from Papercutz, those diligent believers in the freedom of the Press who are dedicated to publishing great graphic novels for all ages. I'm Jim Salicrup, your mild-mannered Smurf-in-Chief, here to make a couple of BIG ANNOUNCEMENTS!

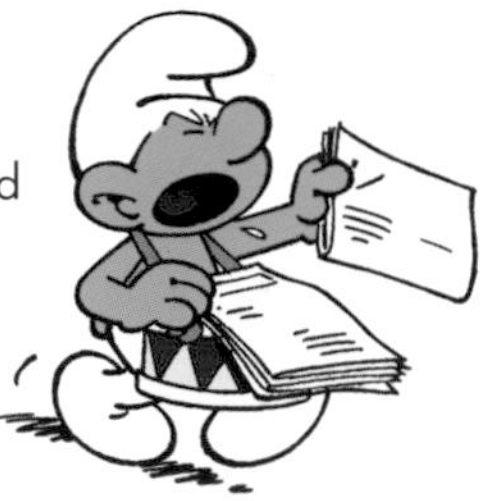

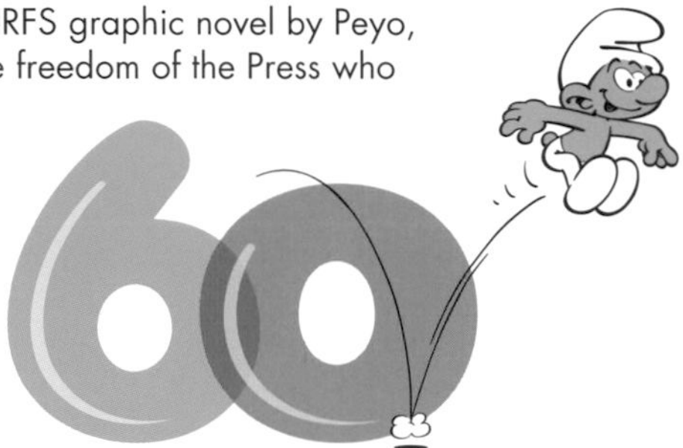
60

2018 was the 60th Anniversary of THE SMURFS, and we celebrated was by publishing THE SMURFS 3 IN 1 #1, which features the first three SMURFS graphic novels published by Papercutz in one deluxe, yet very affordable, edition. It's still available at booksellers everywhere!

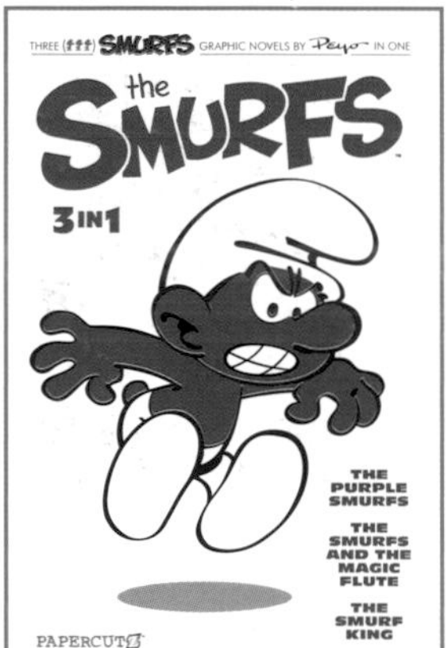
THREE (!!!) SMURFS GRAPHIC NOVELS BY Peyo IN ONE
the SMURFS
3 IN 1
THE PURPLE SMURFS
THE SMURFS AND THE MAGIC FLUTE
THE SMURF KING
PAPERCUTZ

Within the pages of THE SMURFS 3 IN 1 #1, you'll find the story in which the Smurfs made their historic debut—a *Johan and Peewit* adventure entitled "The Smurfs and the Magic Flute." As a special treat for you here, on the following pages, we're publishing a special anniversary story that's a sequel to the very first SMURFS story. The story, just like the Smurf's Anniversary, continues in our next SMURFS graphic novel THE SMURFS #25 "The Gambling Smurfs," available now.

Now, a few words about "The Smurf Reporter," even though this story was originally published 15 years ago, it's as relevant today as it was then. The press needs to be free to tell the truth, and that means no "Fake News." Both the government and the press need to keep each other in check, for, as great comics writer and editor Stan Lee once wrote, "with great power, must also come great responsibility." We asked co-writer Luc Parthoens a few questions about how this story came to be and present that on the next page.

Finally, on behalf of everyone at Papercutz, may I express our eternal thanks to Pierre Culliford, better known as "Peyo," for creating THE SMURFS 60 years ago! And to the Smurfs themselves, Happy Smurfday!

Smurf you later,

Jim

STAY IN TOUCH!

EMAIL:	salicrup@papercutz.com
WEB:	papercutz.com
TWITTER:	@papercutzgn
INSTAGRAM:	@papercutzgn
FACEBOOK:	PAPERCUTZGRAPHICNOVELS
FANMAIL:	Papercutz, 160 Broadway, Suite 700, East Wing, New York, NY 10038

LUC PARTHOENS

While Pierre Culliford, better known as Peyo, is the creator of THE SMURFS, he has enlisted many talented writers and cartoonists over the years to join Studio Peyo to help him meet the ever-increasing demand for SMURFS comics. Since his death in 1992, his studio has completely taken over the creation of new comics featuring THE SMURFS, BENNY BREAKIRON, and JOHAN AND PEEWIT. One such creator, Luc Parthoens, has been playing a major role in contributing to those new comics, and we thought it would be enlightening and interesting to interview him for this volume of THE SMURFS, which features "The Smurf Reporter," which Luc co-wrote with Thierry Culliford.

Papercutz: *Tell us a little about yourself. Where and when were you born?*
Luc Parthoens: I was born October 2, 1964, in Bujumbura (Burundi), Africa.

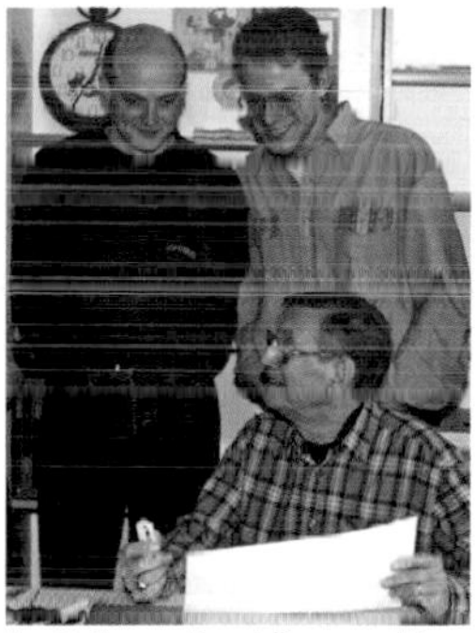
Luc Parthoens, Pascal Garray, and Peyo

Papercutz: *What did you want to do when you grew up?*
Luc: When I was a kid, I was a big fan of European comics and western movies. When I became a teen, I discovered American comicbooks from Marvel and the new generation of the European comic artists such as Moebius and Pratt. From that time on, I knew that I wanted to work in this industry.

Papercutz: *How did you first discover THE SMURFS?*
Luc: My father was also a big fan of European comics. When we lived in Africa, he brought from Europe *Spirou* and *Tintin*, the comics compilation magazines. And it was, of course, in *Spirou* magazine that I discovered our favorite little blue imps. If I remember correctly, it was "The Astrosmurf"...

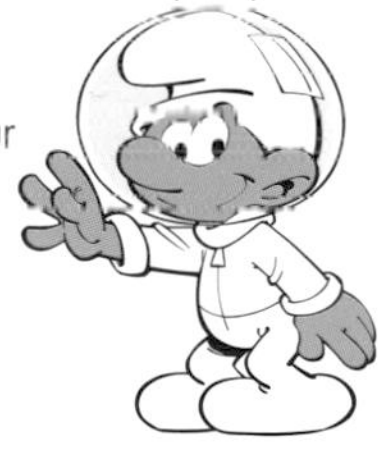

Papercutz: *Did you know Peyo?*
Luc: Yes, the first two years I worked for THE SMURFS, he was still alive. It was a great privilege to know him. He was an outstanding creator, a great narrator, and storyboarder.

Papercutz: *How did you wind up co-writing "The Smurf Reporter" with Thierry Culliford?*
Luc: I had written short comics (8-page stories) with Peyo for the SMURFS Magazine. After he died, by contract with a brand new publisher (Le Lombard), we had to start a new graphic novel. I had some scenarios and ideas that I proposed to Thierry Culliford. We started then a collaboration that lasted seven graphic novels. "The Smurf Reporter" was the fifth...

Papercutz: *What inspired the story?*
Luc: The trigger for the story of "The Smurf Reporter" was the polemic about the role of the paparazzi in the tragic accident of Lady Diana in Paris, a few years before. Thierry Culliford and I thought that it was an interesting start to show how a Smurf could have a good idea to serve the interest of the Smurf community by inventing journalism and became a paparazzi. And concerning the Smurf Reporter's look, our inspiration was Weegee, the American photographer.

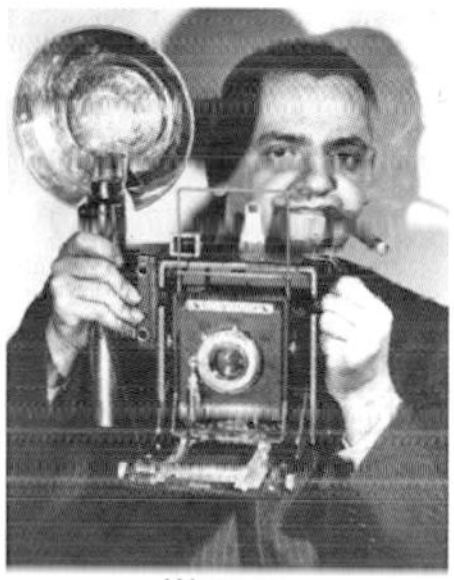
Weegee

Papercutz: *What do you do now with THE SMURFS?*
Luc: Now, I work on the scenarios of our new series of graphic novels "*Les Schtroumpfs et le village des filles*" [Look for THE SMURFS: THE VILLAGE BEHIND THE WALL #2 coming soon from Papercutz] that tells stories of the new Smurf girls characters from the last movie. I'm also on the team that works on our big project of a brand new 3D animated Smurfs TV series that will be on the screens for 2020! I'm really enthusiastic about it, it will be awesome!

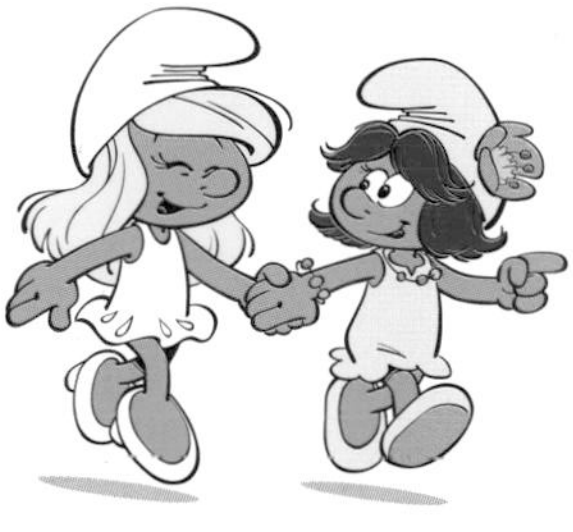

We thank Luc Parthoens for taking time out of his busy schedule to answer our questions.

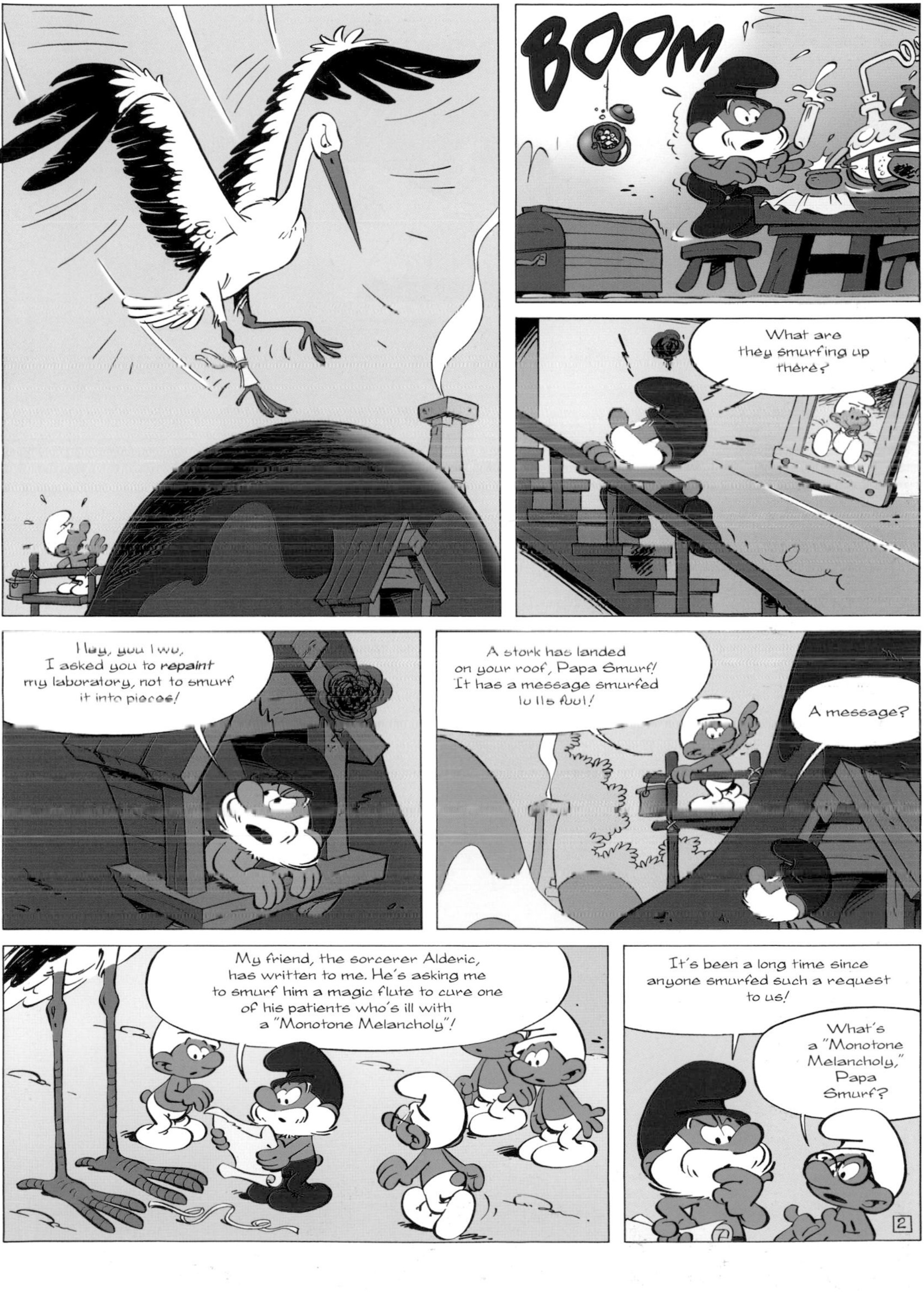
BOOM
What are they smurfing up there?
Hey, you two, I asked you to **repaint** my laboratory, not to smurf it into pieces!
A stork has landed on your roof, Papa Smurf! It has a message smurfed to its foot!
A message?
My friend, the sorcerer Alderic, has written to me. He's asking me to smurf him a magic flute to cure one of his patients who's ill with a "Monotone Melancholy"!
It's been a long time since anyone smurfed such a request to us!
What's a "Monotone Melancholy," Papa Smurf?
2

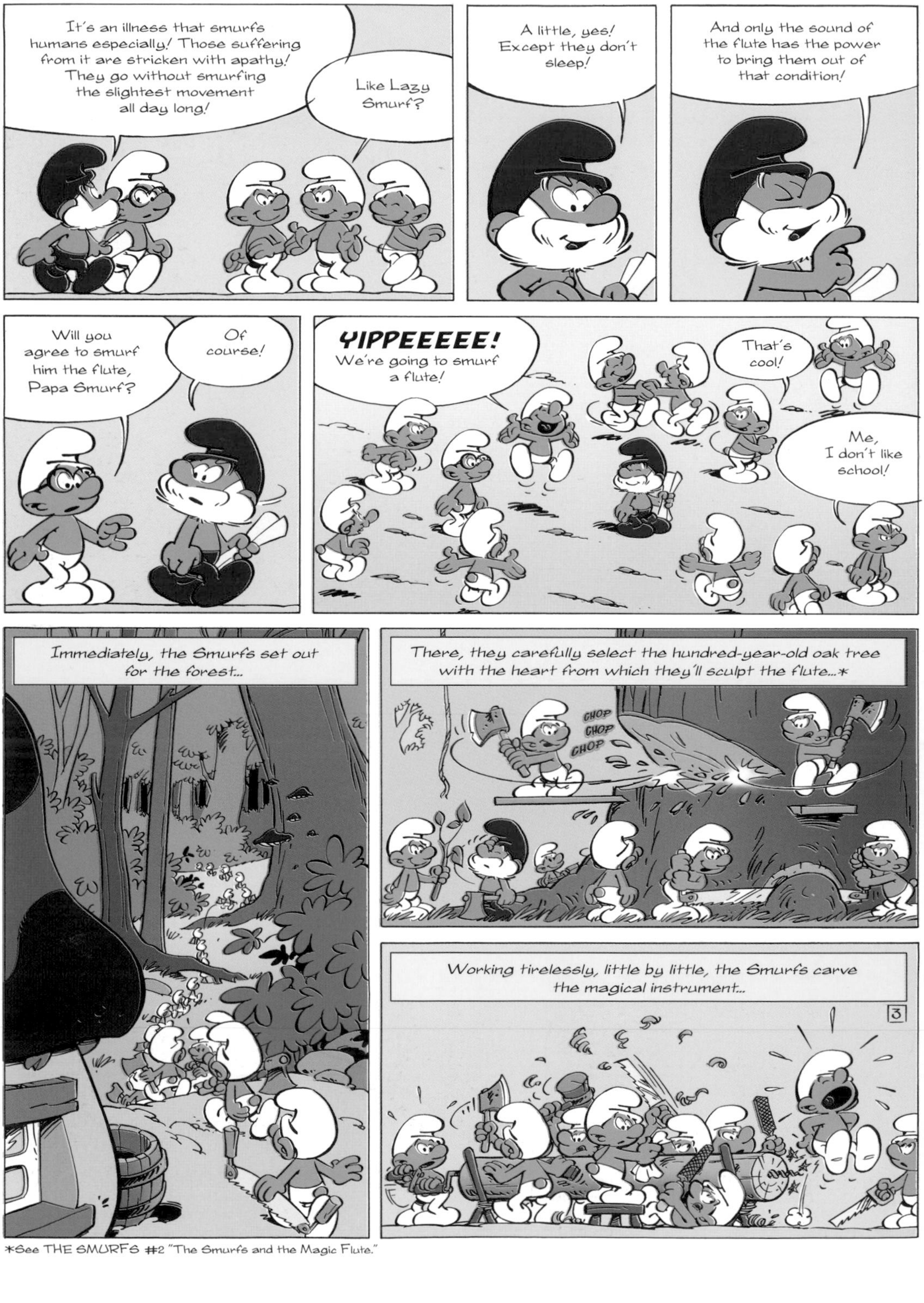
It's an illness that smurfs humans especially! Those suffering from it are stricken with apathy! They go without smurfing the slightest movement all day long!
Like Lazy Smurf?
A little, yes! Except they don't sleep!
And only the sound of the flute has the power to bring them out of that condition!
Will you agree to smurf him the flute, Papa Smurf?
Of course!
YIPPEEEEE! We're going to smurf a flute!
That's cool!
Me, I don't like school!
Immediately, the Smurfs set out for the forest...
There, they carefully select the hundred-year-old oak tree with the heart from which they'll sculpt the flute...*
CHOP
CHOP
CHOP
Working tirelessly, little by little, the Smurfs carve the magical instrument...
3

*See THE SMURFS #2 "The Smurfs and the Magic Flute."

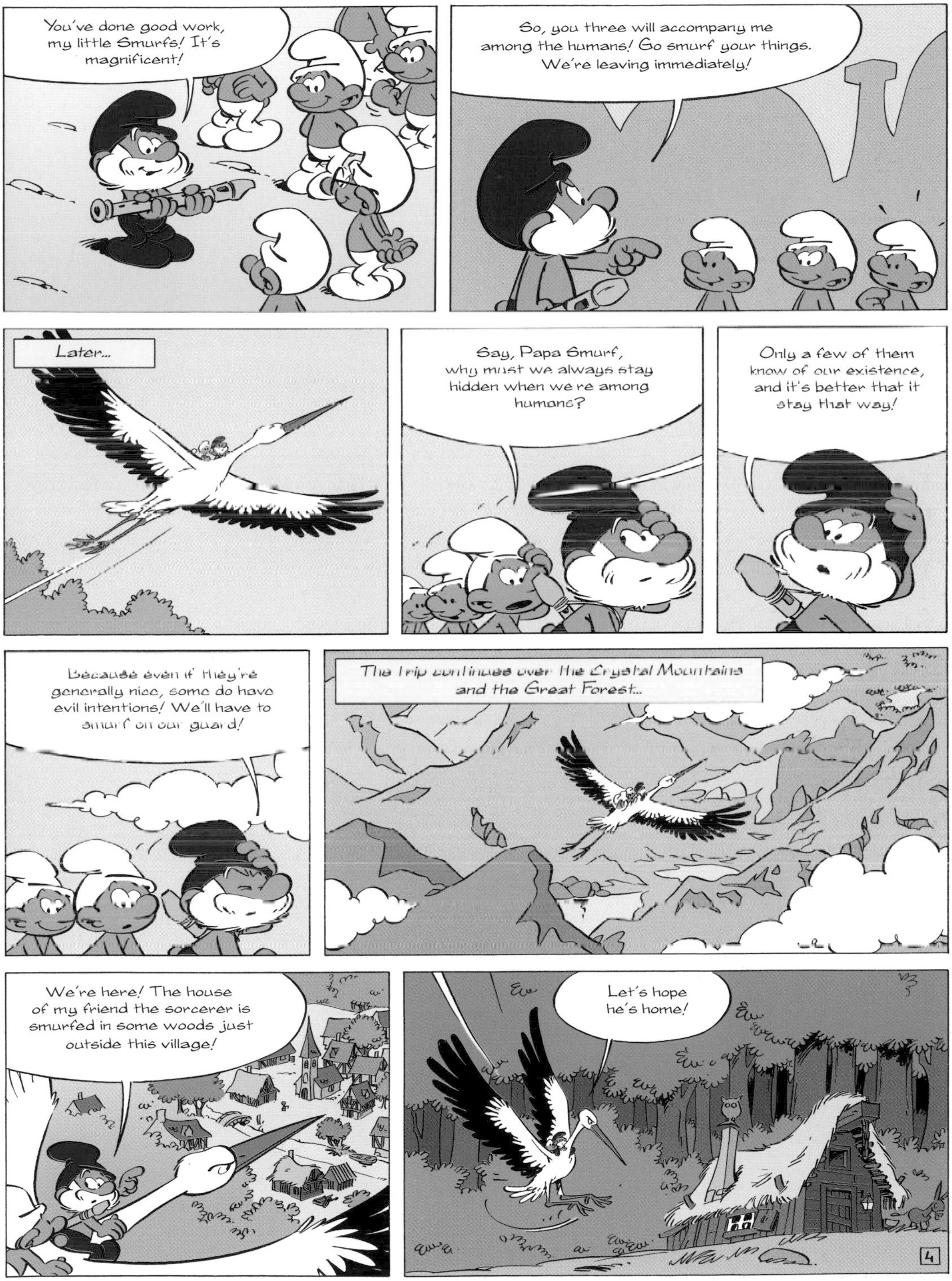
You've done good work, my little Smurfs! It's magnificent!
So, you three will accompany me among the humans! Go smurf your things. We're leaving immediately!
Later...
Say, Papa Smurf, why must we always stay hidden when we're among humans?
Only a few of them know of our existence, and it's better that it stay that way!
Because even if they're generally nice, some do have evil intentions! We'll have to smurf on our guard!
The trip continues over the Crystal Mountains and the Great Forest...
We're here! The house of my friend the sorcerer is smurfed in some woods just outside this village!
Let's hope he's home!
4

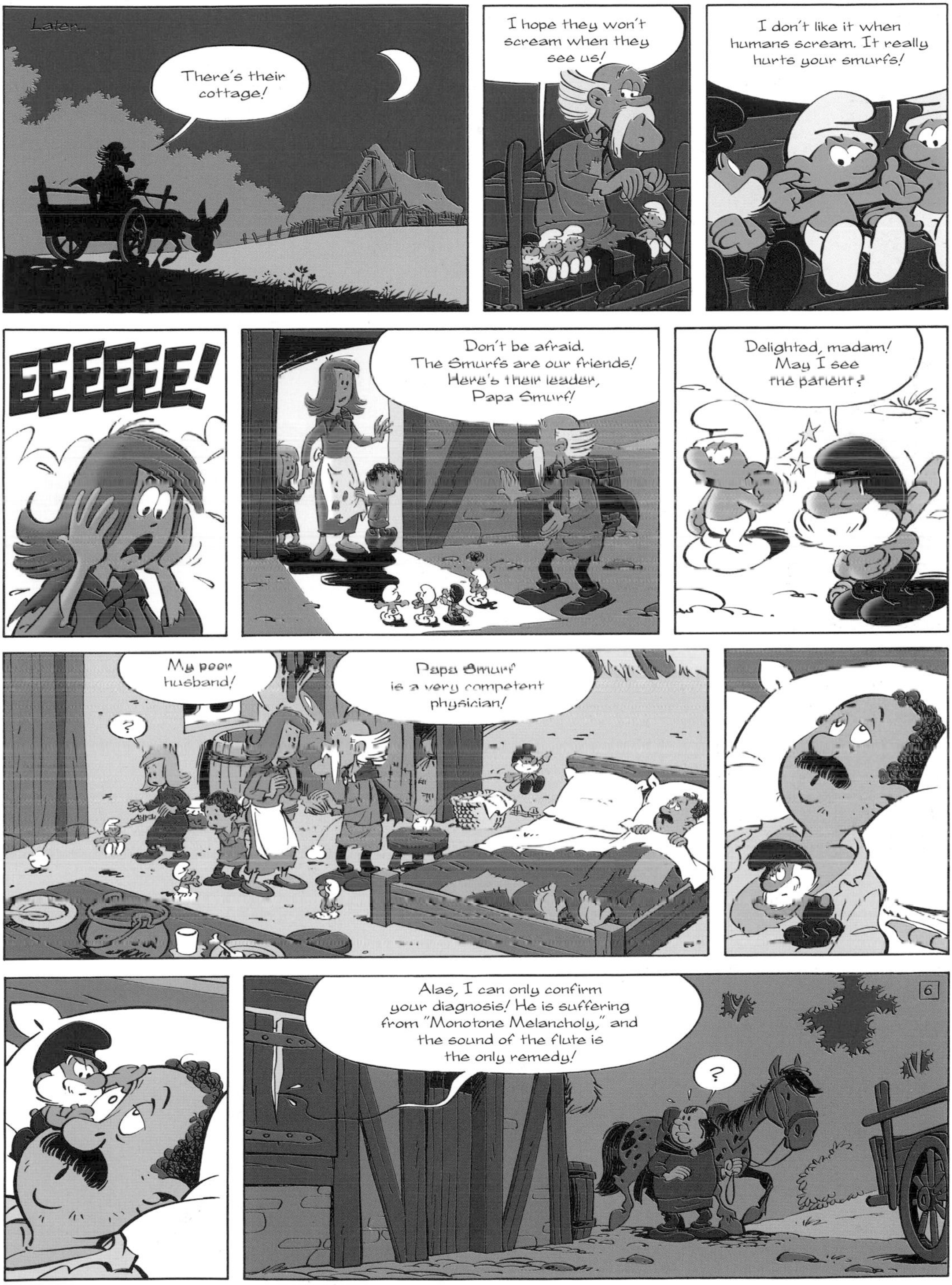
Later...
There's their cottage!
I hope they won't scream when they see us!
I don't like it when humans scream. It really hurts your smurfs!
EEEEEE!
Don't be afraid. The Smurfs are our friends! Here's their leader, Papa Smurf!
Delighted, madam! May I see the patient?
My poor husband!
?
Papa Smurf is a very competent physician!
6
Alas, I can only confirm your diagnosis! He is suffering from "Monotone Melancholy," and the sound of the flute is the only remedy!
?

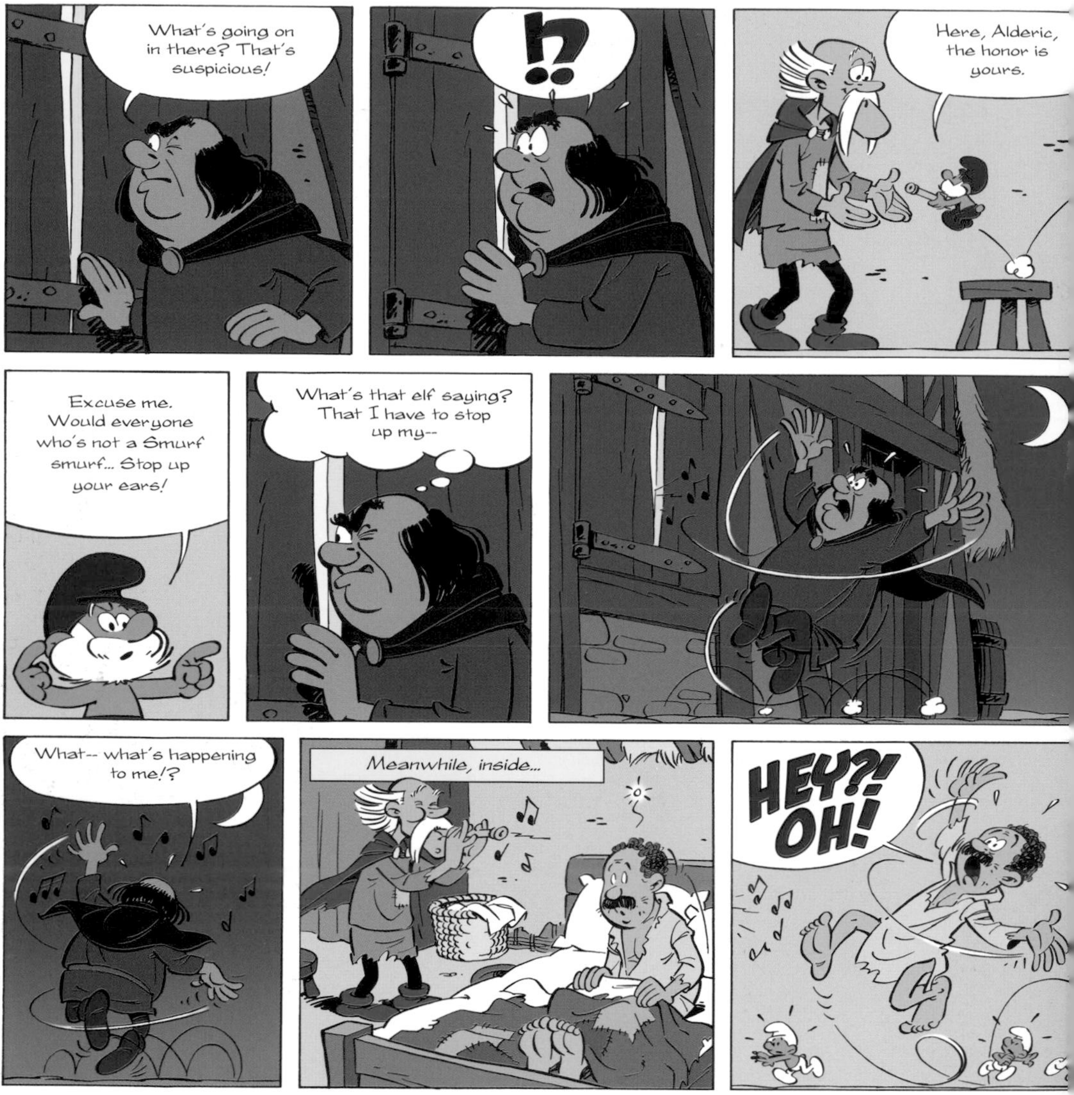
What's going on in there? That's suspicious!
!?
Here, Alderic, the honor is yours.
Excuse me. Would everyone who's not a Smurf smurf... Stop up your ears!
What's that elf saying? That I have to stop up my--
What-- what's happening to me!?
Meanwhile, inside...
HEY?! OH!
STOP! Stop playing! That's enough!
Where am I? What happened to me?
You're cured!
PAPA!
7

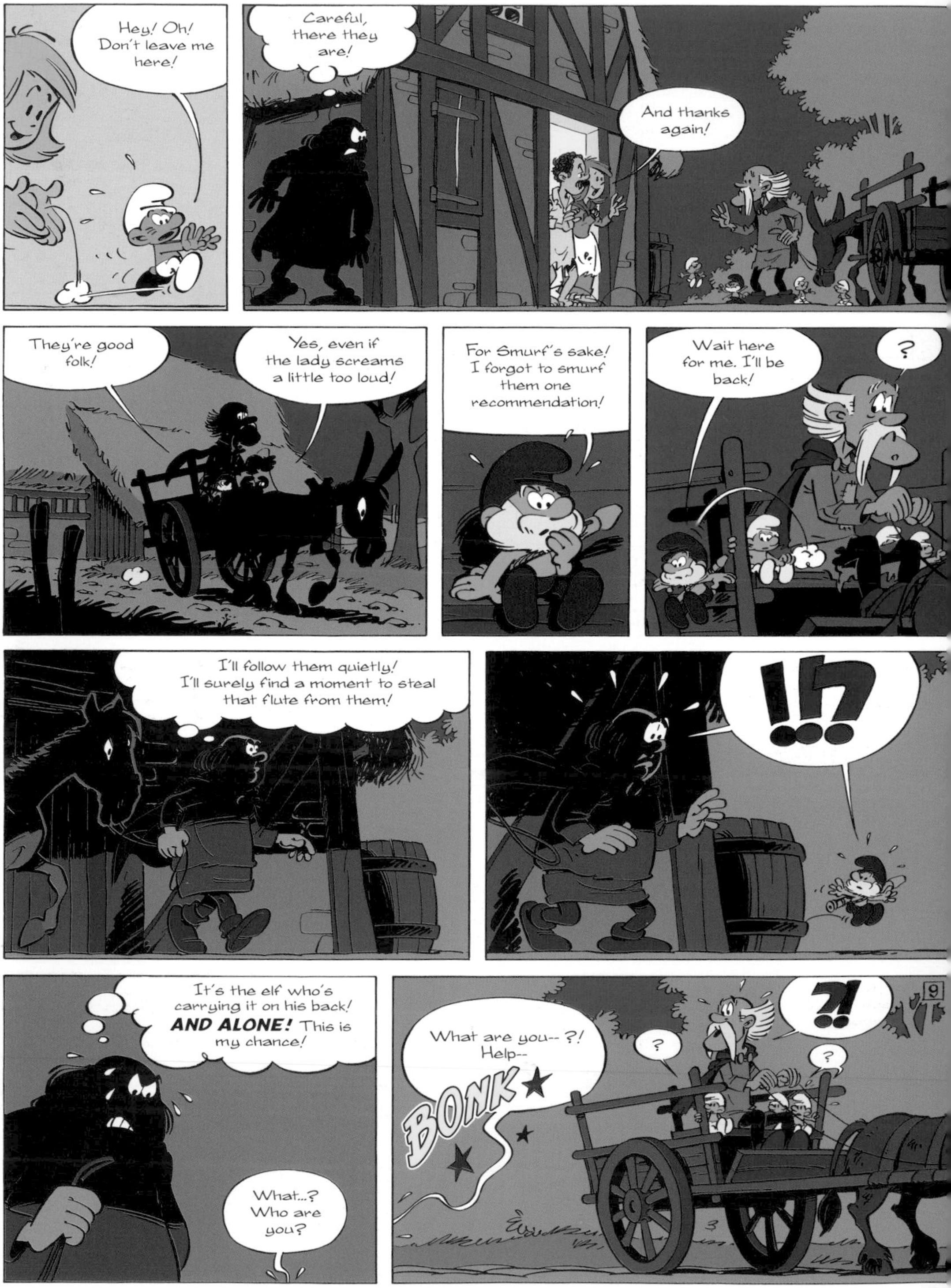

Hey! Oh! Don't leave me here!
Careful, there they are!
And thanks again!
They're good folk!
Yes, even if the lady screams a little too loud!
For Smurf's sake! I forgot to smurf them one recommendation!
Wait here for me. I'll be back!
?
I'll follow them quietly! I'll surely find a moment to steal that flute from them!
!?
It's the elf who's carrying it on his back! AND ALONE! This is my chance!
What...? Who are you?
9
What are you-- ?! Help--
BONK
?!
?
?

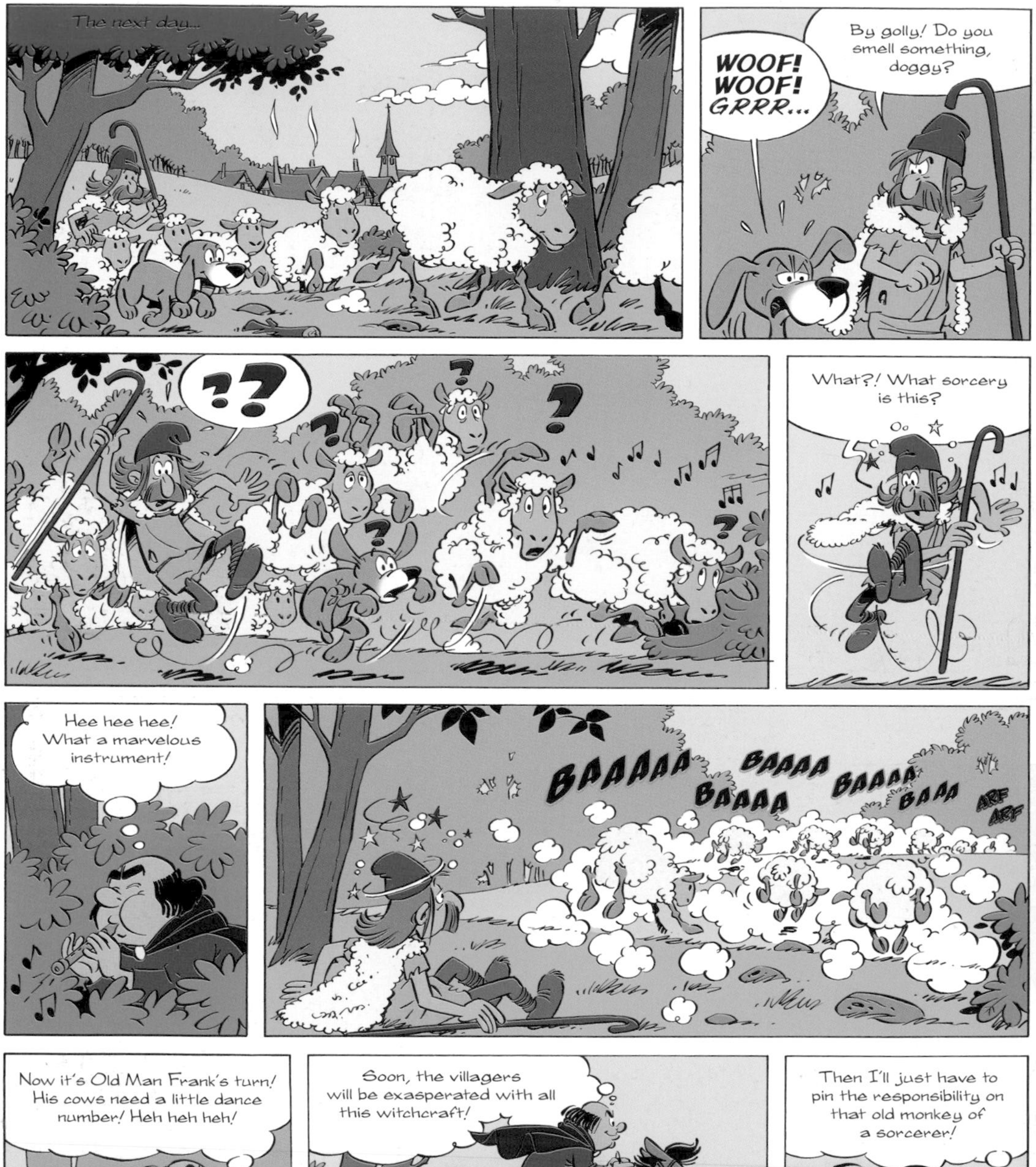

The next day...
WOOF! WOOF! GRRR...
By golly! Do you smell something, doggy?
??
What?! What sorcery is this?
Hee hee hee! What a marvelous instrument!
BAAAAA BAAAA BAAAA BAAAA BAAA
ARF ARF
Now it's Old Man Frank's turn! His cows need a little dance number! Heh heh heh!
Soon, the villagers will be exasperated with all this witchcraft!
Then I'll just have to pin the responsibility on that old monkey of a sorcerer!
11

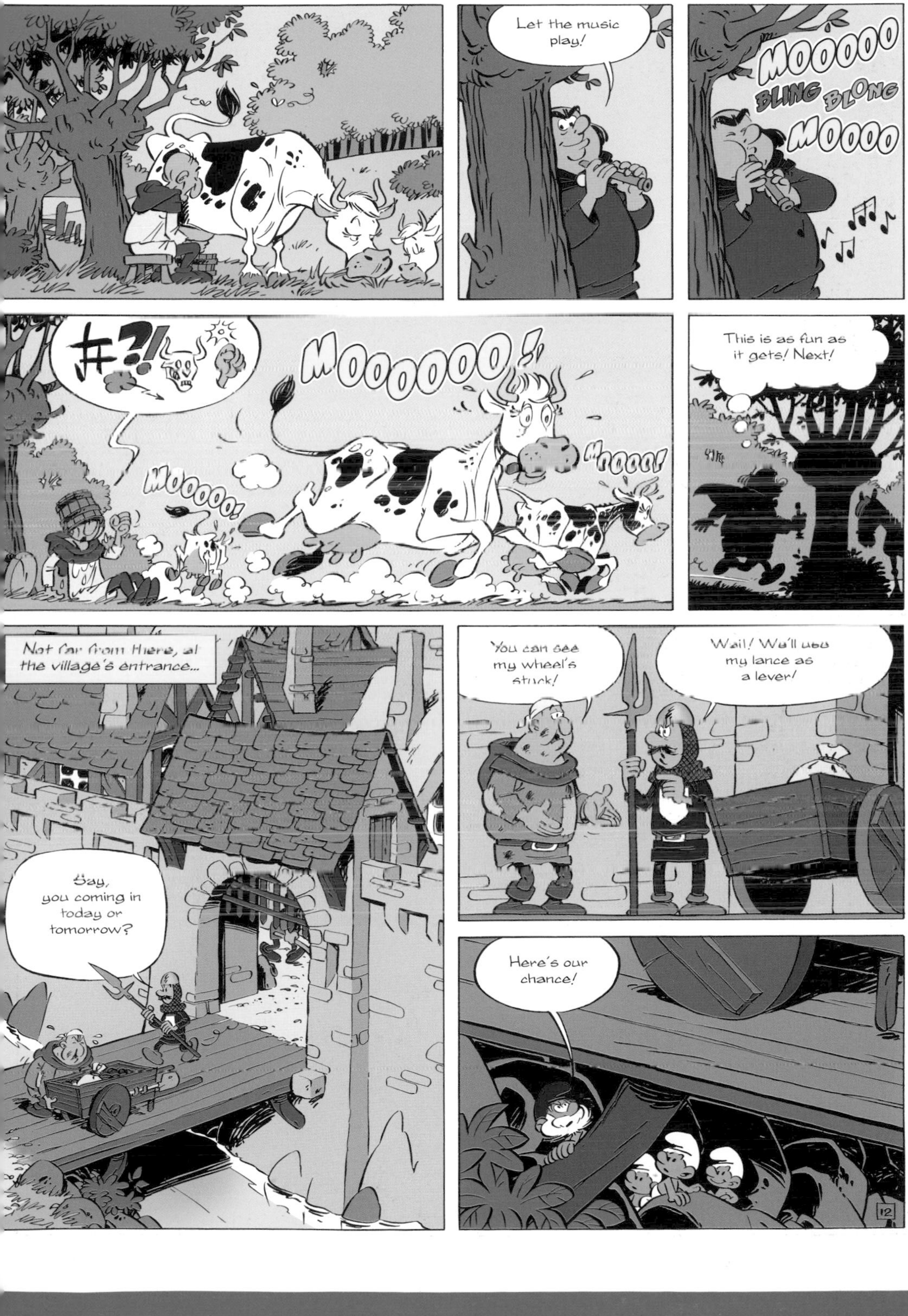
Let the music play!
MOOOOO
BLING BLONG
MOOOO
MOOOOOO!
MOOOO!
MOOOOO!
This is as fun as it gets! Next!
Not far from here, at the village's entrance...
Say, you coming in today or tomorrow?
You can see my wheel's stuck!
Wait! We'll use my lance as a lever!
Here's our chance!
12

THE FLUTE SMURFER concludes in THE SMURFS #25 "The Gambling Smurfs," on sale soon.

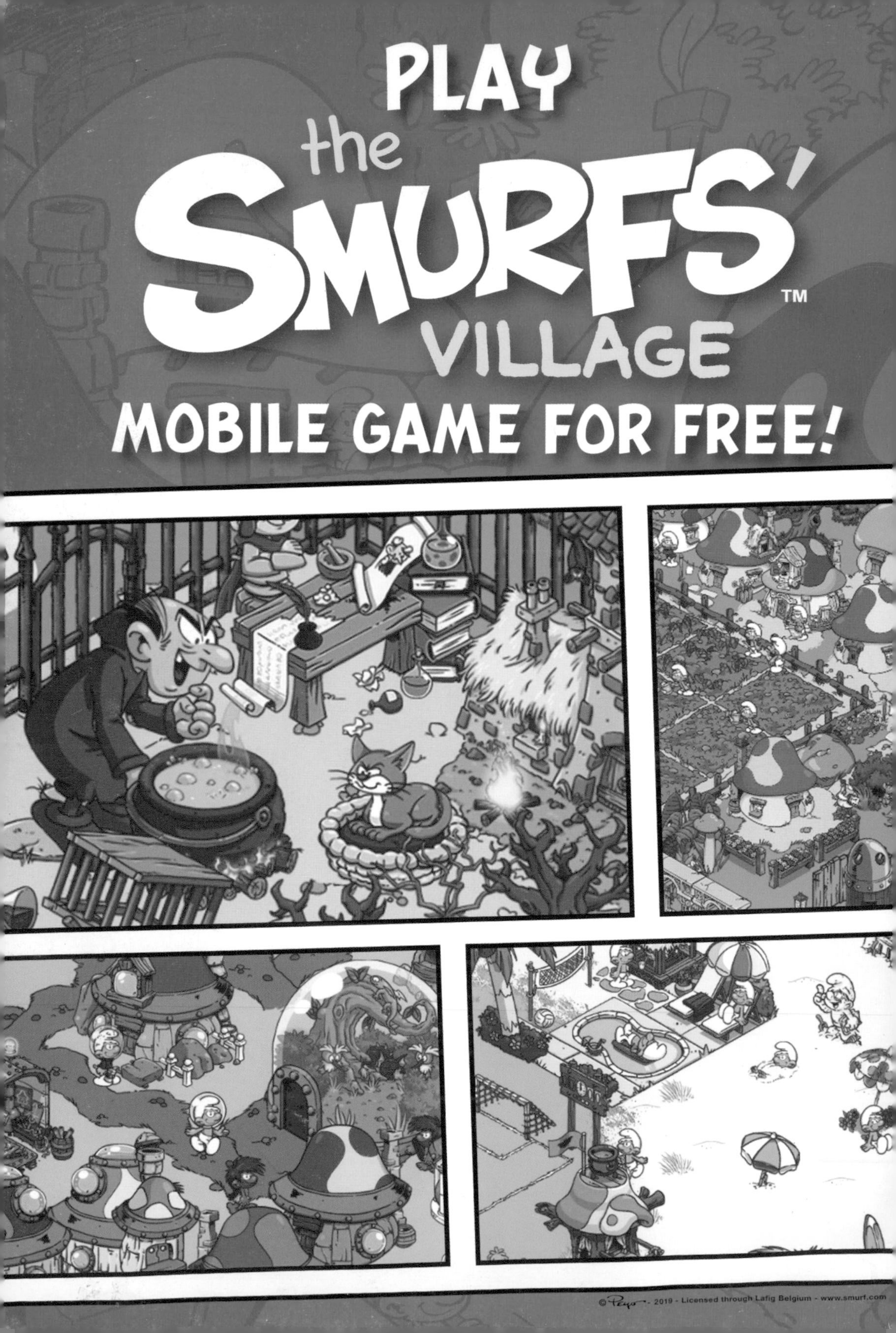
PLAY
the
SMURFS'
VILLAGE
™
MOBILE GAME FOR FREE!
© Peyo - 2019 - Licensed through Lafig Belgium - www.smurf.com